LINDA

Od

ANOTHER SMALL PRESS
No.6

ISBN 978-0-9957127-6-8

Published in Great Britain by Another Small Press, 2025

www.anothersmallpress.net
Cover design by Fine Fine Lines

Linda Cooper is a retired primary school teacher who took up writing when her days in the classroom were over. Over many years she has written a lot, an awful lot. She sometimes says writing is something she needs to do rather than wants, but whatever the reason she loves to put words on paper. More recently writing has been a lifesaver. She has published one book already and this collection of short stories forms her second book. Linda lives in the East Midlands and enjoys her life there. She finds inspiration from the places she visits, the people she meets and the sometimes weird, sometimes wicked and sometimes wonderful things that life presents us with.

Contents

A Dog Is For Christmas

Gone With The Wine

Pitch Perfect

Author's Note

I have written stories ever since I could hold a pencil and as an avid reader I believe it goes with the territory. Throughout my teenage years I wrote a lot of poetry, usually dark and full of angst. During my working years I wrote a lot more upbeat poems, sometimes for special occasions and frequently just for fun. After I retired I decided to join a writing group and that is when I really started to enjoy writing short stories. Since then my life has changed a lot, but I have continued to be a member of various writing groups and the one I belong to now, Fosseway Writers in Newark, Nottinghamshire, is undoubtedly the best and most supportive.

It is through the encouragement of others that I have finally decided to rescue my files of stories from the dark cupboard in which they have resided for many years and bung them all into a book. Some of them are very old, some a lot more recent. Some of them are quite dark or serious and others are totally daft. Some of them I consider to be fairly decent and others make me cringe. But exercises in creative writing require us to experiment with many types of forms, genres and topics, which means we will excel at some and fail at others. But I think most of them want to be in a book.

Consider this collection like an old chest of drawers; one that has been ignored and barely noticed through many years. The contents of its drawers are rather jumbled, varied and probably not in their best condition, but no one has the heart to dispose of them. Someone has finally decided to open the drawers, expose the contents to the light and ultimately sort them into sections. They aren't all the owners best items, the ones that are put on show with pride, but a rather motley and varied collection; maybe faulty, warped, discoloured, out of date, a bit jaded, in bad taste or damaged in some way. Some may be in need of refreshing, patching up or modernising, but better to keep them than discard them to the bin, as they have been around a long time, survived neglect and long to be out there, no matter how imperfect.

Reach into the drawers and see what you can find. It's okay not to open those that hold no appeal, but hopefully there will be something for everyone, no matter what your preference. I hope you can find something in your style and colour that hopefully will raise a smile or bring a tear, instigate a thought or conversation and stay in your memory for a while.

FOOD FOR THOUGHT

Food For Thought

"Waste not, want not" was the creed of Pauline Chamber's family. As ration books became a thing of the past she was reminded daily of how lucky she was to have such luxurious meals put in front of her and how she must always eat every morsel. And nine year old Pauline always did. Sometimes under protest, sometimes to appease, sometimes to ensure she got her fair share of dessert and sometimes so that she was allowed out afterwards. But rarely because she actually wanted to. All the myths surrounding food were part of her daily diet.

'Eat those carrots; they help you see in the dark.'

'Come on, don't just eat the chips. Fish makes you brainy.'

'Drink that milk or your teeth will drop out.'

And the inevitable 'Get those greens down you. They're good for you,' though no one ever explained why.

As the food became more available, the demands to eat every scrap grew. And so did Pauline. At a rate she detested. The school medical was a nightmare. Standing on the cold scales in her too tight navy bloomers she cringed as she heard the doctors' words.

'Mrs Chambers, Pauline is rather over weight for her age. I'd watch her diet if I were you.'

Mrs Chambers was indignant. 'I told him what for,' she related to her husband later that evening. 'Nowt wrong with our Pauline, I said, she's a bonny lass.'

Pauline held back the tears.

Teenage Pauline loved The Beatles, The Stones and the general atmosphere of the sixties. But she hated Twiggy, Jane Asher, Sandy Shaw and any female who could wear the fashions her plump body would not fit into. Rows over food became more frequent.

'What do you wanna look like them models for? They're just bags of bones.'

'Ay love, men like a bit of summat to get hold of,' her dad agreed.

But it wasn't a man Pauline craved for. All she wanted was to control her own diet and acquire the self esteem she felt she lacked due to her size.

'You don't need to diet love; it's only puppy fat.' Pauline knew it wasn't. Tears stung at the back of her eyes.

After leaving home and starting university Pauline believed she would soon be able to shed the excess fat she hated. It didn't happen. With new friends and a hectic social life, Pauline found it almost impossible to stick to a diet and to top it, she developed a taste for the booze. It gave her false confidence and helped her to become the life and soul of every party. Certainly popular, she felt her friends only liked her because they all looked slim by comparison. She constantly compared herself to her sylph like associates and became steeped in self loathing. Her friends tried to reassure her.

'Oh Pauline, stop complaining, you're lovely as you are. Plump people are always so jolly.' Tears welled in Pauline's eyes.

Despite her efforts to diet Pauline walked down the aisle in a wedding dress two sizes larger than she had planned. She knew she was loved by her new husband but how much more would he love her if she were slim? This was the incentive Pauline felt she needed; she would do it for him. But Michael liked to eat out and praised her home cooking and it became even more difficult to abstain from the taboo food she knew she shouldn't eat.

'I don't know what you're worrying about,' Michael reassured her. 'You're fine as you are; plenty to cuddle up to.'

Tears filled Pauline's eyes.

Of course, bearing a son and a daughter caused more weight gain. Pauline grew quite obsessed by her size and constantly talked about her supposed obesity and how happy she would be if she were slim. She never forced her children to eat everything as she had been made to do but found herself forever finishing off their leftovers which didn't help her cause.

'Not hungry, darling? I wish I wasn't, then I wouldn't be so bloody fat.' She sighed, taking away her daughter's half eaten dinner.

'Oh Pauline, give it a rest will you? The kids will get sick of hearing about it. You're fine as you are. A bit of middle aged spread, that's all.'

Tears rolled down Pauline's cheeks as she turned away.

'No potatoes for me, Mum.' Rebecca stated firmly.

Pauline could never have imagined the fear and dread such innocent words would instil in her. She turned and gazed into the hollow eyed, alabaster face of her once pretty teenage daughter, her throat constricting.

'How much further is this going to go? You don't eat enough to keep a fly alive.'

As Rebecca recoiled Pauline instantly regretted her outburst. Oh God, this was all her fault. So wrapped up had she been in her own torment about her size she had failed to notice her sensitive daughter absorbing her misery and unspoken messages about food. Had not seen the signs of an eating disorder far worse than her own.

'Please, darling try,' she begged her anorexic daughter, the tears spilling uncontrollably down her cheeks.

Hush

Marcie's eyes flicked open but the darkness rendered it impossible to work out where she was. Exposed limbs and the cold wall behind her aching back forced her to acknowledge it definitely wasn't at home in bed. The stillness of the air confirmed she was not outside but a penetrating chill added force to the tremors she was having difficulty controlling. Not a flicker of light from any direction convinced her she must be in a basement, attic, cellar or a room with no windows. Either that or she was blind. The disjointed jigsaw pieces of her brain struggled to recall how she came to be here, wherever it was, but no flashbacks or memories could fight their way through the swirling mass of confusion. A tight, sick feeling lifted into her mouth as she tried to swallow the metallic taste of fear. She had no idea whether it was day or night; even if her wristwatch had been on her arm she still wouldn't have known. But she could have put it to her ear, listened to it ticking; the deathly quiet was unnerving her more than the darkness. Marcie had never felt comfortable with silence.

Even in a safe environment the sound of the wind, birdsong, the familiar hum of the refrigerator were not enough; her first automatic action of the day to turn on the radio; drown silence with friendly voices and distracting music. Here, the silence roared; Marcie wanted to fill it with loud screaming, but her voice was paralysed by the same terror that pinned her motionless to the wall. The only thing she could hear was the manic rhythm of the pulse in her ears. She must move.

Crawling, Marcie inched forward over the cold, stone floor, recoiling as her fingers brushed over something warm and sticky. A small part of her felt grateful the darkness prevented her from seeing what it might be, but her ears would have welcomed even the sound of a rat scampering over the floor rather than this unearthly silence. Every second that passed carried the weight of a century of dread. Finally, her hands discovered steps, but the tiny glimmer of hope evaporated like morning dew as a heavy wooden door opened and a flood of light illuminated a silhouette. Marcie's memory returned; she wished it hadn't.

The corners and sides of the jigsaw fell into place, but as yet she couldn't see the whole picture. Shielding her eyes from the sudden glare, she rose to face the woman she had not known existed until yesterday.

'Please,' she begged, her voice barely a whisper. 'Can we talk about this?'

'Shut it,' was the only reply she received. 'Make one sound and there'll be much worse than this in store. Understand?' The door slammed shut as swiftly as it had opened, plunging Marcie back into darkness. Muffled conversation between a male and female faded away leaving Marcie alone once more with her thoughts, her anger and the deafening silence. She recognised the man's voice but knew now he was not the man she'd believed him to be. If she could only turn back time twenty-four hours; a year would be even better.

Almost twelve months ago Marcie met Ben at a party and thought at long last she'd found the man of her dreams. Generous, charming and attentive with an air of mystery that kept Marcie interested Ben had swept her off her feet almost instantly. Their relationship blossomed and intensified, convincing Marcie her future was secure. But then a few weeks ago she'd discovered she was pregnant. Ben's reaction had disappointed and shocked her.

'You have to get rid of it,' he'd stated firmly. 'I'll fix you an appointment as soon as possible.'

'But Ben...'

'No buts, Marcie. I'm not ready to be saddled with kids yet and I don't want anything spoiling our relationship.' Marcie had sensed desperation behind his calm, measured reasoning, but also a distinct feeling that should she not comply, she may never see him again. And that was one thought she couldn't handle.

Reluctantly she agreed; within days Ben escorted her to a private clinic, paying the bill for a termination. Kissing her tearful, frightened face before leaving he promised he'd be in touch once she was home.

The abortion affected Marcie more severely than she could ever have imagined. Emotionally, she wasn't coping; waking each morning to dark thoughts, bitter resentment and a deep longing for her lost baby. Nights of disturbed fitful sleep left her exhausted and weepy; not wanting to face the day ahead. As time dragged by and there was still no word from Ben, her disturbed mental state deteriorated. The heartache for the baby she now longed to hear crying for the first time and the constant nagging voices in her head could be obliterated by the radio no longer. Then, last Monday she'd received a letter.

"Darling Marcie,

I need to see you. Please come to the above address at three 'o clock on Wednesday. There's something I want to show you.

All my love, Ben."

Although angered by his lack of concern for her ordeal, she was relieved to hear from him at last; optimistic they could pick up the pieces and everything would be fine.

But when she arrived at the address, it wasn't Ben who answered the door but an unfamiliar, enraged woman who obviously knew of Marcie. It didn't need the brain of Britain to work out it wasn't Ben who'd written the letter but his wife, whose existence Marcie had never suspected. Shocked and stunned, she was given no time to offer an explanation.

'Bitch,' the woman spat. 'Husbands aren't safe with women like you around.' Marcie opened her mouth to defend herself, but before she could utter a word she was hauled into the house and none too gently pushed down the steps into the windowless, silent room she was now confined in. She could try screaming, make Ben aware of her presence but no longer had any idea how he'd react or what lengths his scorned wife would go to. Sweating and shaking, adrenalin pumping like a mountain spring Marcie brought her trembling knees to her chin, rocking rhythmically. Fear paralysed her to the spot; traumatised eyes gazed blankly into the still pitch of the room and in the eerie silence she had no control over her rampaging mind.

An eternity seemed to pass in the black void before the door opened once more. Marcie's vacant expression barely altered as the figure descended the stairs brandishing a glistening carving knife.

'Get up.' The hissing wife yanked Marcie on to her unsteady feet before prodding her forwards up the steps with the point of the blade piercing her back. Once out of the gloom, malicious eyes bored into Marcie's expressionless face.

'You've been warned,' the voice continued, the knife hovering dangerously close to Marcie's throat. 'Go anywhere near Ben and I'll make sure you never see or hear anything again. Now get out.' Blinding sunlight assaulted Marcie as she was propelled at speed through the front door, but not before she'd heard a familiar noise from the bedroom at the top of the deeply carpeted stairs; a sound that tightened still further every muscle in her body and forced her empty womb to contract painfully.

Her captor, satisfied her vicious threats would send Marcie running like a gazelle pursued by a hungry lion failed to notice the shadowy figure creeping around to the rear of the house or the click of the back door as a deranged Marcie tiptoed past the lounge and ascended the stairs.

'Hush,' she whispered to the gurgling occupant of the wooden cot as she placed a pillow firmly over its face. If Ben preferred to be childless Marcie was perfectly willing to oblige.

Never before had the sound of silence felt so deeply satisfying.

Fair Play

From my bedroom window I watch as the Big Wheel turns for the first time. It's midday on Thursday and the Mayor has just declared the fair open. I know this because I've been present at more fair openings than I care to remember. My home is within walking distance of where the largest fair in England is held for three short days every October. As a child I felt privileged; as an adult I wish I'd lived anywhere but here. Despite its fleeting visit, the fair has been the cause of most of my troubles. The feeling of euphoria I used to experience watching the fair from my window has been replaced by a mixture of bitter resentment, sorrow, regret and fear.

It's a poor neighbourhood where I live with little but the annual fair to brag about, but it's been my home for the best, or should I say worst part of my life. My widowed mother and I moved here when I was a small child; it was all she could afford. I remember gazing in awe through this same window as the fair arrived and I caught my first ever glimpse of the Big Wheel turning.

'Oh Mum, can we go?' I pleaded.

'Of course we can, but there's not much money to spare.'

That first trip to the fair was magical to my six-year-old senses despite lack of funds. The aroma of onions frying, hot peas bubbling, seafood and vinegar mingling exquisitely with the sweet smell of toffee apples and candy floss. Clinging to my Mum on the big horses as I took my first ride, watching in fascination as the indented paper slowly moved to produce the most amazing organ music. Content to hold Mum's hand as we jostled through crowds, my wide, excited eyes transfixed by the multitude of rides and stalls. Later, returning home clutching a coconut in one hand and a hideous ornament in the other; a prize from a stall which at the time I thought stunningly beautiful, the perfect gift for my mother. Drinking the milk from the coconut before bed as Mum treated herself to a brandy snap; the sound of generators, delighted squeals and loud music rang in my ears as I lay in my child's bed cuddling the teddy bear Mum had won on her one game of Bingo.I was unable to drift off as the buzz and excitement still penetrated my windows far into the night, so I sat watching the sky illuminated by a thousand coloured lights, the Big Wheel turning.

Two days later I watched from the window as the fair was dismantled and the Big Wheel disappeared. Later, walking down to the deserted site with Mum; I squelched in mud and churned up grass searching for dropped coins and abandoned souvenirs. This offered a little compensation as the fair hit the road and normality returned. They were simple, happy times.

At eleven I was granted a place at the local Grammar School much to my Mum's delight. She was so proud of me, believing as I did that the future looked bright. We still visited the fair together every year, but as my fifteenth birthday approached I felt the need to exchange her company, slow roundabouts and candy floss for friends, rides that made my stomach flip and alcohol induced bravado with the local lads.

'Mum, can I go to the fair with my friends tonight?' I asked tentatively, sensing she may feel abandoned.

'Of course you can, my love. Just make sure you behave yourself and be back by half past ten. I haven't much to spare but here, take this.' She pressed the last pound note from her purse into my palm, squeezing my hand gently as a gesture of her love. She was such a good mum to me. And I let her down.

As daylight faded, the crowds swelled, the music grew louder and rainbow lights danced in the sky. My friends and I gorged on every gastronomic delight available, swilling it down with a range of alcoholic beverages. Racing from one hair-raising ride straight on to another; still managing to retain the contents of our stomachs as only the young can do. It was after we dismounted from our fifth ride on the Big Wheel that I lost sight of my friends and realised I was drunk, alone and due home in half an hour. The strong, tattooed man who'd been making our carriage rock and our pulses race for the last twenty minutes came to my rescue and offered me black coffee and an escort home.

But what happened in his caravan sobered me up far more quickly than any amount of caffeine and turned me against the male of the species for the rest of my life. Sobbing, I escaped into the cold night air and stumbled home, attempting to compose my dishevelled appearance and mental anguish before facing my mum.

I couldn't tell her about the incident; I felt too ashamed and just wanted to try and push it to the back of my mind. But after three missed periods and a swollen abdomen stretching my school skirt to its limits I had no option but to relay the whole sorry story.

'Oh, my poor darling,' was all she said as she held me close, soft hands stroking me as I told the tale between wracking sobs. 'It'll be alright, we'll manage. We won't let this spoil our lives.'

Mum was wonderful, but my sugar frosted universe had already been shattered, my hopes and dreams for the future melted like snow in early spring sunshine. My grammar school education ended abruptly; Mum decided to stay at home and look after the newborn baby boy I left her to name while I became the breadwinner, working long hours at a local factory. Mum called him Sam after my dad and to all intents and purposes became his mother. I wanted nothing to do with him; he'd wrecked my life.

Time passed like a dull daydream; it was soon time for the fair to arrive again. The trees were on fire with burning colours of amber and gold as I watched the Big Wheel turning from my window, the crying baby in the background a constant reminder of everything I'd lost. I wanted my simple life back.

While mum was out shopping I bundled the brat into his pushchair and set off to the fair with a mission. I'd never asked for a baby so I'd return it to the bastard who spawned it. Let him suffer. I cared not what happened to Sam; I just wanted my mum, my friends and freedom restored. I arrived at the Big Wheel but there was no sign of the man who'd destroyed my world.

'Excuse me; do you know where Joe is?' I asked a nearby fairground worker.

'Joe? You mean Joe McGrath? What do you want with him?'

'I have something for him.'

'You don't want to go messing with his sort missy. He's bad news.'

'I know that ,but could you tell me where he is?'

'The last I heard he was serving a long sentence for attempted murder. He's not been with us for six months now.'

Anger, frustration and fear battled for dominance, but there was nothing I could do except resign myself to the fact that we were stuck with Sam.

'You're better off without the likes of him. Nasty piece of work that one; nothing but trouble from the day he joined us. Nice kid you got there. You go home to his dad and forget about Joe. He's a waste of space.'

I didn't hang around long enough to explain the irony of his advice and I didn't tell my mum about my attempt to rid us of Sam. She reared him as her own without depriving me of attention but I continued to keep my distance, feeling nothing but contempt for him. Sharing DNA with someone doesn't oblige you to like them.

The years drifted by; Sam grew up believing I was his sister but despite the security Mum offered there was something strange about him. Something dark and disturbing even Mum couldn't fail to acknowledge. He was bright; he gained a place at the Grammar School too, which only rubbed salt into my already open wounds. He was moody, often bad tempered; any problems at home and school and he'd fly off the handle then disappear for days until he'd cooled off. I suppose it was a bit of the traveller in his blood, but I didn't really care; the longer he was out of the way, the better as far as I was concerned.

I didn't visit the fair again after that year; the simple pleasures had evaporated like the early morning mists that often enveloped the fair, the memories were too painful. But Sam anticipated each visit with excitement.

As teenage hormones rampaged, Sam became more difficult; sullen and introverted, ensuring he made no friends. Tragedy struck in the year of his fourteenth birthday when Mum passed away suddenly leaving us both devastated but unable to share our personal grief. The gap grew wider, the resentment deeper, Sam spending more and more time alone in his bedroom, isolated from me and his peers. I couldn't contemplate telling him the truth; as no maternal feelings existed there seemed little point. We lived separate lives like a married couple on the verge of divorce but forced to share the same environment. As the fair arrived that October I was very surprised when Sam informed me he was going with his mates; I didn't think he had any.

Sam didn't come home the night of his visit to the fair; in fact as it packed up and moved on he still hadn't returned. I wasn't concerned; his disappearing acts were frequent and of no interest to me. Anyway, a bad penny always turns up as the saying goes. With a bit of luck he'd decided to stay with one of his mystery friends. But, the following week I was summoned to the school where it seemed the teachers were worried about his prolonged absence.

I approached the Head's office with a contrived expression of concern balanced precariously on my face. On entering the room my eyes were drawn to the bowed heads of three tearful youths sitting around the desk of a very stern looking Headmaster.

'Come in, take a seat.' His tone was equally as serious.

'I'm sorry I didn't inform you about Sam earlier,' I attempted to excuse myself. 'You know he has a habit of wandering and I just assumed he'd turn up.'

'I'm afraid it's a little more serious this time and the school is anxious about his welfare. Maybe one of you boys would like to tell Sam's sister what you know.'

The tallest of the three youths looked up but avoided eye contact, an uncomfortable look on his acne-covered face.

'I'm so sorry; we didn't mean him any harm. It was just a joke.'

'Why, what's happened? Where's Sam?' An unfamiliar stirring of concern surfaced from somewhere deep within my buried conscience.

'We invited him to the fair; we spiked his drinks and then ran off when he was on the Big Wheel. He's not been seen since. Everyone thinks he's been kidnapped and we're to blame.' From nowhere, my protective instincts rose from where they had been incarcerated in limbo all these years.

'Don't you think the poor kid's had enough to contend with in life? How could you be so heartless? If anything happens to him it'll be your fault.' I stalked out of the office.

But of course, it wasn't their fault; it was mine. If I'd treated him like a son or a brother, even a human being he wouldn't have become the butt of other people's warped jokes. He could have been a normal lad with a bright future and I'd ruined his chances. Enquiries didn't lead anywhere; who is that concerned about another rebellious teenager leaving home? Sam became just another name on the missing person's list. He's been gone exactly a year to the day now.

As I watch the Big Wheel turning I make a sudden decision. My gut instinct tells me I'll find Sam at the fair not in a shallow grave as predicted by others. When I find him I'll tell him the whole story; maybe we can pick up the pieces and become a family. Maybe it's not too late.

Childhood memories stir in the attic of my mind as I wander alone through the crowds towards the Big Wheel. The scents and sounds are precisely as I remember them and suddenly I'm filled with an unfamiliar feeling of optimism. I know he'll be here; working the fair just as his father did. Something in his blood I guess, but I'm determined to try and sort things out. I had such a wonderful mother and more than anything I want to be one to Sam from now on.

The squeals of delight from the rides fill the cold night air, but amongst them my ears detect a louder, more sinister screaming. As I near the Big Wheel the screams intensify; a terrified, hysterical sound that sends cold shivers down my spine. I'm close enough to recognise the three still, silent bodies of the boys I last saw in the Headmaster's office stretched out on the muddy ground by the ride.

'What's happened?' I ask an ashen-faced bystander.

'Terrible accident. They think that young fairground attendant didn't fasten the bar of their carriage properly. Fell out from the top of the wheel. Didn't stand a chance, poor buggers. What a waste.'

I know without looking but I can't stop myself. I detect a smug, satisfied smile on the face of my son as he is led away by the police. Maybe it's something in his blood that's determined he'll spend the future in the same place as his father, but I will never be sure and never be rid of the guilt that threatens to choke me as I walk away from the fair in turmoil yet again. It's so unjust that I'll never have the opportunity to make amends. But then, as my mum used to say, no one ever said life was fair; if you'll excuse the pun.

Goodbye Good Guy

Richard walked away from the hospital totally stunned. "Three months to live." The words echoed repeatedly in his head. On impulse he drove to the marina and spent a few hours on his precious boat, knowing he would never sail again. He then headed for home in a daze and went into the bathroom.

Lizzie's afternoon of passion with her lover was rudely interrupted by her mobile phone demanding to be answered.

'Leave it,' he whispered, nuzzling her neck.

'I can't, it might be important.'

'Emma. Hello darling. How are you?' Lizzie recognised her daughter's voice but it lacked the usual enthusiasm. 'What's the matter?'

As Lizzie drove to the hospital she felt surprisingly calm. Although married to Richard for twenty five years the news of his death had barely shaken her. Not that she didn't care; just not in the way she should about a good man; hardworking, loyal, trustworthy and reliable. That was the problem really; he was just too bloody boring. Lizzie craved excitement, adventure, not the predictability of a mild mannered saint. But this was totally out of character; Richard was just not the sort to top himself. Why would he? They had everything; a luxurious house, cars, a boat, a holiday home abroad and a pleasant, if somewhat bland, relationship.

Her five year affair with Ed had been kept a secret from everyone, so it was not a problem. Richard spent a lot of time at work and Lizzie made sure nothing altered in her attitude towards him ever since the affair began.

It had been easy really; Richard trusted her implicitly, never questioning her motives or activities. She'd had no intention of leaving him; life was far too comfortable to warrant any such drastic action. Living with an amenable, if predictable, gentle man like Richard became tolerable; she'd intended to plod along as she was, enjoying the comfortable lifestyle she had with Richard and supplementing her other needs with Ed, who she loved passionately but who could never keep her in the manner to which she'd become accustomed. Well, maybe now the situation had resolved itself; fate could be very kind.

Lizzie managed to squeeze a few tears as she entered the morgue. She couldn't help thinking Richard looked about as interesting in death as he had in life when identifying his body.

'Yes, that's him. But why would he commit suicide?' she asked the doctor. 'There were no problems; he had everything to live for.'

'Well, Mrs Goodman, it appears your husband was suffering from a rare form of cancer. The prognosis was not encouraging.'

Lizzie was shocked, a little sorry even, but relieved that he had his own personal reasons for ending his life. She had no reason to feel guilty.

'That's so typically Richard.' Lizzie wiped her eyes with a tissue. 'Unselfish, right to the end. But why didn't he tell me? How long had he known?'

'He was only told this morning. Maybe he couldn't face the thought of a lingering, painful death.'

'No, it would be me he was thinking about. I know Richard. He wouldn't want to be a burden. He was always so considerate and kind and never a man to cause trouble. I shall miss him.'

Well, it was the truth to some extent. she *would* miss him; just as she had missed her pet rabbit when it died just after her seventh birthday. She'd soon recovered from that and it was replaced by another almost immediately. Lizzie already had a replacement in mind for Richard, but there would have to be a respectable time lapse before she introduced Ed into her life and home. This had to be handled more delicately than just introducing another rabbit to the old hutch after it had been disinfected.

Lizzie managed to manifest the required emotions throughout the funeral and in the weeks that followed, inwardly raring to start her new life. Ed, though not the placid type that Richard had been, maintained patience and sympathy. He did love Lizzie; even more so now she had inherited everything.

'I think we should go away for a while,' Lizzie suggested. 'Take the boat somewhere, enjoy a long holiday and then we can arrange a suitable courtship when we return.'

Ed was happy with this arrangement. The following Saturday he drove them to the marina, loaded up the boat and turned the ignition key, eager to begin their first vacation together. The explosion was heard many miles away and debris from the boat still evident weeks later.

The inquest concluded that Richard had known of Lizzie's relationship with Ed and knowing he had no future had decided to ensure they would not benefit from his death.

Emma wiped the tears from her pale, drawn face as she walked from the court. She may have inherited her father's good looks, but her devious, opportunist disposition was even stronger than her mothers. She had known of Lizzie's affair with Ed for several years but had said nothing for she loved her gentle father dearly and did not want to see him hurt or create a situation where the family might break up. Her resentment bubbled inside for a long time but on hearing the news of her father's suicide it reached boiling point. Her father would definitely have earned a place in heaven but she had made sure her deceitful mother and her lover would rot in hell for eternity. Turning the corner she smiled with relief that the ordeal was finally over. Everything, except the shattered boat, now belonged to her. But she'd always hated sailing anyway.

Perfect

'Not today Frank, please. It's too hot.'

Frank glares at me, his perfectly shaped brown eyes penetrating my thoughts, sending a shiver of fear down my spine.

'You know what I told you Colleen; you'll wear the gloves until the day before my parent's anniversary party. Go on; get to the shops before all the best stuff's been picked over.'

'But Frank, I look ridiculous wearing gloves in this weather. Everyone stares at me as if I'm crazy.'

'Remember when everyone stared because you were so amazingly flawless? That's the woman I married and that's the woman I want back. No more arguments and pick my suit up from the cleaners on the way back.'

There's no point continuing the debate. I'm tempted to tear off the stupid gloves and deposit them in the nearest waste bin but know what would happen if I did. It sounds ridiculous I know; a grown woman being dictated to in this day and age, but not everyone has a husband like Frank.

My thoughts drift into the past as I make my way to the small shopping centre in town, doubled under a heavy load of self pity. Head down, eyes focussed on the paving stones but still painfully aware of the questioning glances of passers-by. What sort of girl wears gloves in the middle of summer? Ask *him* I want to scream.

Frank and I enjoyed a whirlwind romance at university and I foolishly wanted a wedding ring on my finger before anyone else succeeded in snapping him up. I remember the best man at our wedding describing us as the "perfect couple." Within weeks I realised Frank's idea of perfection was to dominate our lives and that he'd go to twisted, bizarre extremes to satisfy his ambitions. It was not, as I'd imagined, the perfect partnership and obvious pretty early on who would dominate.

Just a few weeks after the wedding I discovered my husband was not the unblemished man I'd believed him to be. We, or rather he, purchased a compact new house on a private estate. Frank insisted he'd earn enough to keep us both so I'd not sought employment. I thought it rather sweet and old-fashioned of Frank; wanting me to stay at home and was quite prepared to channel my energies into creating domestic bliss. One afternoon, satisfied all chores were completed for the day I sat watching an old weepy on the television when Frank burst through the door like a shell from a cannon.

'There's some dust on the hall table,' he bawled almost hysterically, his perfect, full lips trembling as if he'd discovered a corpse. I tried to laugh it off, but after a while I realised our home must be as spotless and sterile as an operating theatre to avoid Frank's wrath.

Then the day I burnt the evening meal; it was only a sharp clip on the cheek, but enough to convince me Frank has a real problem. He punished my incompetence by arranging for his mother to stay with us until I'd learnt to cook real family meals. I've never had time for my mother-in-law and partly blame her for Frank's behaviour; raising him to believe he's the perfect male specimen and nothing is good enough for him, especially me.

My cooking improved as the relationship deteriorated, but providing the house was cleaned daily from top to bottom and there were no culinary disasters, life was tolerable. After the birth of our second child however, Frank's obsessive criticism turned personal.

'You're out of shape, Colleen. You've put too much weight on and your figure's getting flabby. It won't do, you know.' Tears stung my eyes, but I wasn't brave enough to argue that it wasn't his perfect body that had endured the trials of pregnancy and childbirth.

Under Frank's supervision I was forced to take up rigorous exercise routines; producing top quality meals for the family whilst existing on rabbit food myself. Both my weight and self-esteem plummeted, but that was not to be the end of it. For my next birthday, Frank presented me with an appointment for cosmetic surgery, silicone implants. He may as well have written "Your tits are too small," on the accompanying birthday card. There was no pleasing this man it seemed.

I know, I should have left him, but you tell me where an unemployed mother of two young children turns? And I suppose, deep down, I hoped Frank would soon be satisfied and all this would stop.

Physically, I was nearing the perfect image Frank desired, but mentally and emotionally I was falling apart. Had cigarettes or alcohol been allowed in our home I suspect I'd have turned to them to calm my frayed nerves. Instead, without even realising, I began to bite my fingernails. Only lightly and occasionally at first, but soon seizing every opportunity to sink my teeth into what was left of my nails and the flesh surrounding them. Of course, it wasn't long before Frank noticed, almost causing a cardiac arrest. Hence the gloves; I've had to wear them now, day and night throughout the longest, hottest summer on record. It's been so uncomfortable and embarrassing.

All the time I'm loading the groceries into my basket I can feel the eyes of the check out girl and other customers on my covered hands and I can't escape the shop fast enough. Similar reactions at the dry cleaners where I hastily pick up Frank's suit; it didn't need cleaning, it was immaculate when I brought it in, though not in the eyes of Mr Impeccable. How I wish something or someone would damage his perfect image for once.

Two weeks later we sit around his parent's perfect mahogany dining table, surrounded by immaculate crockery and food. The discussions rarely include me; I'm just here as a decoration, complete with impeccably manicured and painted nails. Frank seems happy, his mother gloating over his faultless appearance and ignoring eye contact with me. I'm bored and frustrated; I feel resentment simmering like a boiling kettle underneath my calm, polished exterior.

Later that night, Frank rolls his perfectly toned, tanned body onto mine. There's a moment's hesitation before he announces, 'Aren't you glad I made you beautiful again? Maybe you could do with a tummy tuck though.'

My scarlet talons find his face in the dark. He will carry the scars from the scratches on his cheeks for the rest of his life and I will carry on *my* life without him. Perfect.

Beyond Belief

'Have you booked my birthday bash yet?' I ask Ray before setting off to work.

'No, I'll do it now. How many people?'

'Twelve, including us; I hope they have a table left.'

'Have you invited our Sylvia?'

'Oh God, do I have to? You know what she's like. Can't I enjoy one social occasion without her?'

'Aw, don't be like that Val. She means well.'

'That's a matter of opinion. I suppose I'll never hear the last of it if she doesn't come. Probably put a curse on me. Make it thirteen then.'

Ray's expression alters immediately. I let out an exasperated sigh. 'What now?'

'Well, you know what Sylvia would say about that. Thirteen people sit down at a table and one will die before the year is out.'

'See, this is just what I mean. Everything has to revolve around her and her stupid ideas. Okay, I'll ask Jill from work to join us; anything for a quiet life. Make it fourteen. Got to run, see you later.'

Dashing out the front door I almost trip over the cat basking in the morning sunshine. 'Shift, damned useless article. You'll be the death of somebody one day.' It gives me a withering glare and saunters away. I hate cats.

Driving to work I feel familiar resentment bubbling like hot lava. To describe Sylvia as superstitious is a gross understatement. Her whole existence is based on legends, rituals and old wives tales. To make matters worse she continually inflicts her opinions and idiotic beliefs on all my family and friends. Sylvia is Ray's older sister; unmarried of course. She tells people she's still waiting for the right man to come along. According to her he will walk towards her on a Thursday, wearing a green tie, but only after she has spotted ten blue cars followed by a red-haired girl wearing purple.I suspect she may have a long wait and heaven help any poor man who ends up with her.

"Weird" is hardly an apt adjective for Sylvia; I have no time for her and her bizarre views. Unfortunately, the rest of her family, including Ray, hold her in awe. They claim she's gifted, something to do with her being born on Friday the thirteenth during a thunderstorm or some trite rubbish. Load of old poppycock, but I try and keep it to myself for Ray's sake, although the way they treat her with kid gloves irritates me. I could tolerate it if it was just the average apple-a-day, four-leafed-clover, not-walking-under-ladders or opening-umbrellas-in-the-house type of stuff, but Sylvia's beliefs go much further and venture way into the realms of the ridiculous. Even the revolting rabbit's foot she refuses to be parted from for fear of ill luck had to come from the left hind leg of a rabbit killed during a full moon by a cross-eyed person. Sylvia tells us this is exceedingly lucky although thankfully, as yet, she's spared us the details of how she acquired it.

At seven 'o clock that evening thirteen of us sit around the restaurant table awaiting the arrival of Sylvia who strolls in thirty minutes late.

'Sorry to keep you waiting,' she apologises lamely. 'I came out without my amber beads; can't go anywhere without them, I feel unprotected. Of course when you return to your house to fetch something you have to sit down and count backwards from seven hundred to ward off evil spirits. Did you know that?'

Once my polite guests have raised inquisitive eyebrows there is no stopping her. There follows a strained evening during which Sylvia instructs us we must always eat fish from head to tail, cut bread in even slices, not cross knives or drop cutlery for fear of various plagues and disasters. Even our natural bodily functions are dissected and analysed by Sylvia's bottomless pit of trivial mumbo jumbo. My cousin accidentally bites her tongue during the main course and is immediately chastised by my dear sister-in-law, who proceeds to announce in a loud voice that this only happens if you have recently told a lie. Gina, my dearest friend, spills pepper on the table, which according to Sylvia symbolises an argument with your best mate. Cheers. The ensuing sneezing caused by the spilt pepper allows Sylvia to delight in informing us 'Sneeze on a Friday, sneeze for sorrow.' Our pregnant guest has her side salad deftly removed by Sylvia who tells us, with a smile, that lettuce can induce an early labour. The bundle of joy known as Sylvia ensures that a good time is *not* had by all.

I'm so stressed by this stage my left eye begins to twitch, which of course does not go unnoticed by our resident clairvoyant.

'You be careful, our Val. A twitch in the left eye foretells of a death in the family.' Fortunately for her, all sharp implements have been removed from the table.

Doom and gloom settles on the guests like a heavy winter snowstorm and I can almost hear the collective sigh of relief when the waiter arrives with my birthday cake and the bill. Pent up energy and frustration allow me a plentiful enough supply of hot air with which to extinguish the thirty candles in one go.

'Ooh Val, you've blown them all out. You can make a wish now.' Sylvia broadcasts. 'But you mustn't tell anyone what it is or it won't come true.'

'Oh, believe me, I wouldn't dream of it,' I reply, praying Sylvia doesn't come out with some anecdote about the fate of those who smile insincerely.

The company departs rapidly, Sylvia leaving only after reminding me not to fasten my coat up wrongly or I will receive a visit from an unwelcome guest. A little late I fear.

The drive home is tense; my indignation at having my birthday ruined mingles in the cold night air with Ray's protective instincts towards his sister. If Sylvia's prophesies bear any truth then during our journey her ear must be about to ignite. Not her left one either. It's been like this since the start; Sylvia to my mind is the only jinx on our marriage.

In the early days of our relationship I found Sylvia eccentric yet mildly amusing. As time passed it became obvious she was to play a larger-than-average part in our future and I grew increasingly more agitated as our wedding day approached. I had planned on making my own wedding dress in a dreamy cream satin, but Sylvia had soon put a stop to that.

'Don't you know it's unlucky to make your own dress? And you must have heard the old rhyme "marry in white, you've chosen right." I had no doubt Ray was the perfect man for me but was beginning to wish his sister had been born into a different family, preferably in another dimension.

A fortnight before the wedding Sylvia presented us with her gift - a black cat. For good luck she said. I hate cats. The following week I caught the thing eating Whiskas out of my left shoe, the team mate to the outrageously priced Gucci pair I had purchased for my big day. My scream brought Sylvia onto the scene where she explained it was a tradition to bring good luck to the prospective bride and groom. If it hadn't been so pathetic it would have been funny. From then on there was nothing but conflict between us.

I wanted a May wedding; it didn't meet with Sylvia's approval.

'Marry in the month of May and you'll surely rue the day. I'm only thinking of your happiness you know.'

I'd have settled for a traditional Saturday later in the year but that didn't suit her either.

'You know what they say, Val. Thursday for crosses, Friday for losses and Saturday for no luck at all. I just want the best for you.'

I wasn't even allowed my favourite red roses in the bouquet. According to folklore it's bad luck and Sylvia was having none of it.

So, I walked down the aisle in my hired white dress and stained shoe, carrying a bunch of chrysanthemums on a cold wet Wednesday in November. Sylvia beamed proudly from the front row of the church looking far happier than I felt.

'And don't go dropping the wedding ring our Raymond,' she whispered as I stood nervously by his side. 'Or the marriage will be doomed.' With Sylvia as my sister-in-law I was beginning to think there might be an element of truth in that.

As we left the church she handed us a silver horseshoe. 'Make sure you place it open end upwards or your luck will run out. Oh, and put it in your bedroom to ward off nightmares.' I resisted the temptation of telling her no nightmare could ever possibly compete with her.

Before stepping into the car (right foot first as instructed by Sylvia) I tossed my wilting bouquet over my shoulder, making sure it was way out of reach of Sylvia. I was only thinking of that poor, unsuspecting young man in the green tie, honestly.

The honeymoon was wonderful but returning to live with Ray's family soon became unbearable and I eventually persuaded Ray we needed a place of our own. Of course, Sylvia ensured choosing a new home became as complicated as a mission to Mars. Every place we viewed had to be assessed for suitability by Sylvia. The house number had to be even, the front door had to open onto the street and the bedroom had to face east. Left to Sylvia every estate agent in the district would go bankrupt in a matter of weeks.

Eventually, we secured a property to suit Sylvia's requirements although our departure was delayed, as according to her ladyship, it's unlucky to move in April. The house was old and in need of renovation but as long as it distanced us from Sylvia I didn't care. Naturally, she had to assist on removal day.

Leaving the men to do the heavy lifting inside I stepped out into the warm June sunshine and decided to tidy up a little outside.

'Ray, where's the dustpan and brush?' I shouted up the stairs.

'Oh, I've got rid of that,' Sylvia's voice drifted through the kitchen window. 'Never take an old broom along when you move. Throw it out and buy a replacement. New brooms sweep clean you know.'

Humphing, I decided to dig up the sprawling creeper attached to the side of the house. I hate Ivy.

'What are you doing?' A distraught-faced Sylvia appeared at my side as if by magic. 'You must keep the Ivy; it'll protect the house from witchcraft and evil.' I made a mental note to visit the nearest garden centre and ask about plants to ward off unwanted relatives. I threw down my spade and decided to make tea for us all.

'Well, I'm sure you'll be very happy here,' Sylvia predicted, raising her cup of camomile tea as she knocked three times on the wooden tea chest.

I'm quite convinced Ray and I would have been perfectly content in our new home if Sylvia hadn't been a constant thorn in the flesh.

A week after my birthday Sylvia pays one of her many uninvited and much too frequent visits to our home. It's a bitterly cold day and snow has been falling for most of the afternoon.

As she sips her elderflower tea and forces her latest theories and puerile notions upon us, the cat wanders into the lounge carrying a flapping bundle of feathers in its mouth.

Sylvia gasps in horror. 'Oh God, a dead bird in the house is a sign of an impending death. Get it outside quickly.'

'Well, it's that bloody cat you gave us that brought it in.' I release the bird, thankfully uninjured, into the winter sky and assist the cat, none too gently with my foot into the garden, cursing under my breath.

'Aw, don't be hard on him, Val. It's freezing out there. You make sure he's inside before you go to bed.'

'Don't worry about that psychotic fur ball,' I retort. 'It would find its way back here from Land's End. It has a charmed life; nine in fact.'

Eventually Sylvia leaves us in peace. I flop down on the sofa with a sigh of relief, only to discover her disgusting rabbit's foot lodged between the cushions.

'Oh hell,' I shout to Ray in the kitchen. 'Sylvia's left her good luck charm. I'd better see if I can catch her, she'll have a seizure if she discovers it's missing.' Better to venture out in the cold than risk another visit from her tomorrow.

I race out the front door. The temperature has dropped dramatically and the snowfall is now covered with a rock-hard, lethal blanket of ice. Looking down the street I see the cat dash out into the road, hear the screech as Sylvia slams on her brakes, then watch in open-mouthed horror as her car skids, and careers into a six-foot solid brick wall.

Five days later, on a wet Friday afternoon I gaze into the deep hole that will be her resting place for eternity. Guilt weighs down on me as heavily as the sodden earth that will soon cover her coffin. Although my life will now be free of Sylvia I know I will never escape the feeling that somehow I am responsible for her premature demise. For people who, like me, scoff at superstition and the gift of second sight I have only one piece of advice. Just be careful what you wish for.

BATTLE SCARS

Forget It

'Oh my God,' mumbled Pam as she rolled over, trying to recall what day it was. 'Never bloody learn will I?' she asked the mattress. 'Too much lager, too many fags, not enough sleep; they'll put that on my gravestone.'

Despite the good soaking she'd indulged in the previous night she had not slept well and a weird nightmare had disturbed her during the few short hours she had spent asleep. It would be difficult to forget it. But, as predicted, another day had arrived, the bright sun reminding her that, despite her hangover, there was no way of avoiding it. 'T.G.I.F, at least,' she remarked sleepily to the pillow she was feeling reluctant to leave.

'Come on you lazy cow,' she chided herself. 'Up. One, two three.'

The room span as she became vertical, her surroundings a blur.

'Where are you? Come out wherever you are,' she yodelled to her absent spectacles. Never on the bedside table where she was convinced she always left them before falling into bed at night, or rather early morning. One night she would stay awake and catch them in the act; deliberately scuttling furtively to some obscure hiding place. Groping around on the floor she managed to locate them inside her pink furry slipper. The left one; God knows where the right one was.

'Another batch of brain cells lost in the night, ten steps nearer dementia,' she grumbled to the carpet. 'Never used to lose things when I was younger; knew where everything was in those days. But then I didn't need bloody glasses either,' she concluded as she placed them haphazardly on her nose and stumbled to the bathroom.

'Oh Christ,' she cursed at the oval shaped mirror. 'Do you have to be so honest?' A zombie sporting a wild afro hairstyle peered back at her, sunken cheeks, black circles under the eyes and at least two dozen more wrinkles than yesterday. Thirty more grey hairs too. A guess; she hadn't the ability to count them.

'I must "dye" this weekend,' she told the mirror. 'If I can fit it into my exciting, imaginary social calendar.' Still, at least the weekends were a time to relax and she didn't have to go through these rituals to make herself look semi human. She could be the slob she truly was. Forget it all.

Her mind jumped forward to Monday.

'Morning Pam. What did you get up to this weekend?'

'I dyed,' she would reply.

'What, again?' would come the predictable answer. 'You'll go down in the record books for the most number of reincarnations at this rate.'

Maybe the Monday she didn't turn up at the office they would all wonder if she had really died. Maybe she would, all alone in her flat, unwashed and wearing no make up. It was bound to happen at a weekend wasn't it? How would it happen? Alcohol poisoning? A fire from a carelessly discarded cigarette? An accident caused by her inability to see without her absent spectacles? A heart attack maybe? She hoped so. 'Whatever, make it quick,' she pleaded to the Almighty who would decide her fate, wherever he or she resided. 'Not dementia please, anything but that.'

'And what are you grinning at?' she snapped at the false teeth floating in the glass by the sink. 'Oh time, thou art so cruel,' she mused as she glanced at her watch. Oh hell, that time already? She had a major renovation job to perform yet before setting off to work. She'd be late. She hated being late, but often was. Probably be late for her own funeral.

'Sorry I'm late, folks' she would announce in a muffled voice from her coffin. 'Couldn't decide what I wanted doing with my gorgeous corpse, never was good at making decisions was I?' Burial? No way. It would be worse than being trapped in the office lift; confined in a cold dark space for eternity. Cremation? Forget it. She had a fear of fire, wasn't hell the place of everlasting flames? Science would have no use for her pickled organs so donation was out. God, why did her mind insist on pondering these imponderables?

'Concentrate.' she chastised the zombie. Teeth in position, the next half an hour was spent indulging in every cream, lotion, potion, spray, powder and cosmetic that her meagre income could not afford to buy. But at least there was a visible improvement.

'Nice face, shame about the cellulite,' she complained, feeling her thighs jiggle as she hurried back to the bedroom.

'Decisions, decisions,' she muttered to the row of outfits hanging inside the cluttered wardrobe. Maybe she'd have a sort out this weekend, get rid of all that stuff that reminded her of her slimmer days. 'Charity shop for you lot,' she threatened her size twelves. 'Serves you right for shrinking.' Another blessing that came with age; the development of excess flesh where it wasn't invited. Pam squeezed into a classy grey two-piece but then realised she had forgotten to put on underwear first.

'Oh hell, nine steps nearer dementia,' she shouted at the drawer, yanking it open and grabbing a pair of the recently acquired big cotton pants she'd been forced in to purchasing. Terrible to think that if she died in a road accident on the way to work and was rushed to hospital she would be exposed to the world in these things. The shame of it.

'Death again,' she admonished her thoughts. 'Always come back to it don't you? What's the point dwelling on it? What's the alternative? Eternal life? God, what a thought." She slammed the wardrobe door.

Grabbing her coat and bag she swiftly left the flat and made her way to her car. After a frantic search she realised she had no car keys,

'Oh, shit, eight steps nearer dementia,' she complained to the front door as she reopened it. 'I'm turning into my bloody mother, I knew I would.' Visions of a future shuffling around town in fluffy slippers and a green woolly hat, wondering what she'd gone into town for in the first place filled her head,

Finally locating the keys, she settled into the driver's seat and switched on the radio.

'And now, here's "What's it all about, Alfie?" for all you Cilla fans out there' announced the D.J. 'Then we'll be returning to the News on this beautiful Saturday morning.'

'What?' gasped Pam 'Saturday? Oh my God. Dementia has arrived.'

Choosing Eve

I'm Eve. 29. Looking for my Soulmate. I'm honest, perceptive, ambitious and creative. I love nature, gardening, food and travel.

It's worth a shot.

Monday.

Swipe

Matthew. 31. Generous, Attractive, Energetic. Enjoys walking and films.

Review - Stingy, Grotesque, Slothful. Has a strange concept of what is attractive and uses Photoshop. No car, no umbrella, no manners. Walked in the rain to the cinema, no offer to pay for tickets or popcorn. Fell asleep before the end of the film and started snoring. Left him there. A definite no.

Tuesday.

Swipe

Tony. 28. Enthusiastic, Attentive, Sophisticated. Enjoys eating out and technology.

Review - Apathetic, Ignorant, Uncouth. Turned up in ripped jeans, undersized T shirt and crocs. Insisted on eating at his favourite restaurant. Guzzled two McFlurries, belched after every burger and farted after fries, all the while scrolling on his phone. Departed quickly after being called his chicken nougat. Never again.

Wednesday

Swipe

Winston. 30. Adventurous, Trustworthy, Reliable. Likes driving and music.

Review - Deranged, Reckless, Narcissistic. Turned up late with no apology. Suggested a drive in the country. Exceeded speed limits, failed to signal, ignored red lights and blocked lanes. Accelerated continuously like some wild psychopath accompanied by heavy metal blaring from speakers, horn honking, brakes screeching and obscenities as a result of his frequent outbursts of road rage. Absolutely not.

Thursday.

Swipe

Travis. 32 Rugged, Passionate, Charismatic. Enjoys dancing and wine

Review. - Hairy, Horny, Hideous. Tipsy and slurring his speech even before reaching the nightclub. Polished off several bottles of cheap plonk before hitting the dance floor. Wandering hands, grinding hips, intrusive groin and filthy mouth. Tripped over a table leg and left in an ambulance. No chance.

Friday

Swipe

Felix 26 Extrovert, Optimistic, Amusing. Loves gaming and reading.

Review - Vulgar, Cantankerous, Immature. Suggested coffee at a new board game cafe in town. Launched into telling a series of jokes from a children's book, laughing manically after each one, followed by a raucous snort. Played games by his own rules, cheated and had a hissy fit every time he lost. Deliberately knocked over his strawberry milkshake on the Monopoly Board and was asked to leave. Nothing doing

Saturday

Swipe

Steve. 40. Mature, Interesting, Patriotic. Likes Martial Arts and Social Media

Review - Pensioner, Aggressive, Xenophobic. Leathers covered the many offensive tattoos on his sizeable frame. Doesn't own a shaver or a deodorant. Downed several beers at his local pub while he ranted about the downfall of society and what he would do to those he considered to blame. Attempts to alter the conversation resulted in disinterested grunts. No way.

Sunday.

Her phone is turned off.

There is nothing out there for her. It's a barren desert, devoid of respectable men.

She's already expelled one snake from her life and has no need for another.

Today she chooses Eve. Chooses peace, security, freedom. Chooses to care for her garden and nurture her soul. Chooses fruit from the tree to bake apple pie for one.

She feels blessed, contented, tranquil.

Helping Hands

Rodney gazed through the rain streaked window, mentally landscaping his small plot of land. Gardening suited his quiet, gentle nature. Still deeply saddened by the death of his mother but mature enough to realise that life must go on, Rodney felt sure he'd made the right decisions. It was a small comfort to know he'd have a little more time between shifts to devote to his favourite hobby.

Chestnut Grove lay in a secluded area just outside town; Rodney felt confident he'd be happier here. Too many memories lingered at the old house where he'd spent his entire life. From potty to middle-aged paunch, his lovely widowed mum had been there for him, but now it was time to face the future alone.

Following the aftermath of his loss, Rodney decided change would help him cope best with grief. This new residence and a much needed career move, he hoped, would be the start of a totally different existence. On Monday he'd start his new job; he prayed Mum would smile down on him with pride from wherever her tender soul now resided. If heaven existed he knew she'd be welcomed with open arms; she'd been a good woman all her life and had always kept his best interests at heart, even if she did have an annoying habit of always knowing what was best for him. Well now, he'd make his own decisions.

Just as he visualised the cabbage patch at the bottom of the garden, his doorbell rang. He'd only moved in a few days ago so was surprised anyone should call this soon.

A frail, tearful old lady perched on his doorstep, frozen like a small bird on the edge of a precipice. Rodney felt a fresh stab of grief as he observed the similarity to his dear, departed mum. The same watery blue eyes, the gentle laughter lines and the damp silver hair straggling round her delicate face in a fuzzy halo.

'Can I help you?' he enquired in the soft tone he'd reserved for his mother.

'I'm sorry to bother you,' her wavering voice replied. 'I've locked myself out and I wondered if you'd be able to help.'

'I'll do my best. Where do you live?'

'Just down the road, number sixteen. All my neighbours are out so I didn't know what to do.' Rodney smiled; how vulnerable and easily flustered the elderly are.

'Well, don't stand there trembling, come in where it's warm. Here, I'll help you with your shopping trolley.'

'Thank you, you're very kind. I was just off to the shops when I realised I'd left my key in the house. If you could help me get back in I'd be ever so grateful. There's a bedroom window open if you've got a ladder. I'm a bit too fragile for scaling heights these days.'

'Not in a hurry are you? Time for a cuppa?'

'Oh, that would be lovely. I don't get pampered very much these days. My name's Gladys by the way.'

Over tea and biscuits Rodney enjoyed hearing Gladys's little anecdotes and stories from her youth. He was pleased to be able to give a bit of time to someone like his mum, who was obviously lonely and not very well off.

Rodney fetched his ladder and escorted Gladys to her home. He climbed into the back bedroom of the house, closed the window behind him and let Gladys in through the front door.

'Thanks ever so much Rodney. I don't know what I'd have done without you.'

'No problem, you sure you'll be alright now?'

'Yes, I'm fine. I'll just get my key and then I'll be off to the shops. Thanks again.'

'Anytime,' Rodney replied, squeezing her bony hand; the paper-thin skin so like his mums. 'If you need anything you know where I am. Take care now.'

The following Monday morning, Rodney presented himself at his new workplace. He felt proud of his smart uniform and ready to face his first assignment. His new boss approached and placed a file on his desk.

'Okay Rodney, let's see what you make of this. On Saturday, a house in Chestnut Grove was burgled while the owners were away for the weekend. Here's a list of what's been taken. There's no sign of a forced entrance and no witnesses. All we have to go on is a sighting of an elderly lady leaving the premises late in the afternoon pulling a heavily-laden shopping trolley. It looks like we may have a pilfering pensioner on our hands.'

The boss seemed highly amused, but Rodney's voice stuck in his throat like peanut butter and the phrase, "Rodney, you plonker" reverberated around his brain.

It seemed his mum was right again; she'd always said he was too gullible to be a policeman.

Anything You Can Do

As I turned the corner I saw him standing in a circle of light underneath the lamp-post. I wasn't positive it was him, but there was something about his superior pose, his cut above the average suit, the not-a-hair-out-of-place appearance that drew my attention. It was supposed to be my night out with the lads, but I was early so I decided to drive around the block and take another look.

Slowing down as I passed the lamp my suspicions were confirmed. It was him all right. Spencer bleeding Simcock. I'd not set eyes on him since leaving school. but he'd barely changed. Didn't look a day older either, but then, being Spencer he'd probably been born with an extra gene that prevented him aging. Maybe he was immortal.

I'd known Spencer since starting school at five. My mum had assured me I would be the tallest, strongest and brainiest boy in my class and I'd believed her, but then neither of us had accounted for Spencer Simcock. You know the sort; anything you could do he could do better. Whatever you had, or did, he had one bigger and better or had done it with knobs on. Mr Superior, Mr Perfect, Mr Pain in the Arse. Throughout my whole school career he'd made me feel about as much use as the Pope's testicles.

I remember our first playground encounter well. Wanting to impress him I'd approached him one morning play time. Six years old and already painfully aware of his supremacy.

'Hello, I'm Michael. Fancy a game of marbles?'

He looked down his nose, firstly at me and then at the treasured collection of marbles I held in my grubby hand.

'Is that all you've got?' was all he said. Never believe that sarcasm is lost on children. He condescended to play and walked away with every one of my precious marbles jangling in his pocket, alongside his superior ones. I never did win them back and I never forgave him. I spent years trying to get one over on Spencer bleeding Simcock but never succeeded.

For every "very good" I received on my school work he received an "excellent." For every blue ribbon I won on Sport's Day, he walked away with the red one. I was always a star in the school plays, but he always landed the leading part. I played one of only two xylophones in the school band, he played the one and only drum. Even when I broke my arm I returned to school to find he'd broken both, gaining him more sympathy, attention and plaster area for signatures.

Nothing altered when we both transferred to Grammar School. If I achieved ninety-nine marks in an exam it was always topped by his perfect one hundred. For every B plus I earned, he was awarded a straight A. (A plus wasn't around in those days but it wouldn't surprise me if they later invented it in his honour.) If I scored a goal in football, he'd score a hat trick. When I later became a prefect he became Head Boy. And so it went on. Spencer could also have his pick of the girls; they all seemed to go weak at the knees when he was around. While the rest of us stood around with our tongues hanging out, too frightened of rejection, Spencer was carving notches on his bed post as fast as gaining all his other qualifications. It seemed the man was faultless and I lived in his shadow, bubbling with resentment.

School was a long way in the past, but I'd never come to terms with always being second best to Spencer. I'd done pretty well for myself; good job, comfortable home, nice car and the best wife a man could wish for. Rachel and I met at a party a few years ago. It turned out she went to the same school as Spencer and I, but being several years younger she didn't remember us. But she soon became painfully aware of my animosity towards the infallible Mr Simcock.

'Why can't you just forget about him?' she'd ask every time I related one of my bitter tales from the past.

'I don't know. It just gets to me. He was just too bloody good to be true. I reckon he gave me a lifelong inferiority complex.'

'Well, you're the number one man as far as I'm concerned,' she'd reassure me, but I always recognised a glint of pity in her eyes.

I backed into a space beside a flashy red Porsche. One glance at the personalised number plate and it was obvious he'd done well for himself too, but I wasn't going to let that put me off. I feared that old feeling of inferiority would return as soon as I spoke to him, but this was something I had to do.

'Spencer,' I shouted, feigning enthusiasm as I approached him. 'I thought it was you. How are you mate?'

'Michael, old chap. Not seen you in years. I often wondered what happened to you. Fill me in.'

'I'm doing well. Went to Manchester University after school and studied law. I'm a solicitor now.'

'Hey, I went into that field too. Studied at Cambridge. I'm a barrister. Of course he is.

'Where you off to anyway?' His snooty accent is already irritating me.

'Going for a drink and a curry with some friends from work. Always do on a Wednesday when the wife goes to her Keep Fit class. How about you?'

'I'm meeting an old girl friend.'

"Oh, never married then?"

'No, never found the right girl.' Well, he wouldn't would he? Not until they market a blow up doll with IQ.

'Don't know what you're missing mate. Been married five years now. Fabulous wedding, honeymooned in Mauritius. Wonderful.'

'Oh, what a coincidence. I've got a villa there.' Of course he has; probably got one on every planet in the solar system.

'You should get hitched Spencer; can't beat it in my opinion.' I flashed him my best, happily married, domestic bliss smile.

'Maybe. We'll see. Must get together some time. I think this is the girlfriend.' He raised an arm to wave at the approaching figure.

I turned to look and recognised her instantly, despite the distance. I watched as my beautiful Rachel returned the wave and smile. I remained silently rooted to the spot as she approached.

'Well, hello Rachel,' Spencer drooled as she came within earshot. 'You're looking good.'

'Hi darling, you're looking pretty tasty yourself.' She smiled at Spencer, and then turned, winking, before enfolding me in her arms.

The expression on Spencer's face will stay imprinted on my mind for the rest of my life.

It had been Rachel's idea. She's smart as well as beautiful. She'd checked out our old school on one of those Social Media websites and found Spencer's notes posted there. She'd contacted him, making out she remembered him and suggested meeting up. He'd responded quickly, admitted he'd always had a crush on her at school and would be delighted to meet. I'd had my doubts the plan would work, but it looked like we'd pulled it off.

Rachel turned to a very confused and for once, defeated looking Spencer.

'I take it you remember Michael. It slipped my mind to mention I'm married to him, and believe me he's worth ten of you. You may think you're superior to the rest of us, but I wouldn't touch you with a barge pole. Compared to Michael, you're nothing."

My ego, along with other things, expanded to hitherto unknown dimensions. Linking arms with Rachel I grinned at Spencer, a deep feeling of satisfaction spreading through me. At last, I'd got something he couldn't have. Sweet.

Lone Spirit

'That's as far as I go.' Jess came to an abrupt halt then turned to look at me, a determined expression on his face. 'Follow the footpath and you'll come to the house. You're on your own now.'

I stared along the path into the gloom. The early winter sunset cast a pale watery light over the trees, creating ghostly shadows of the tall conifers. I shuddered. Turning to look at Jess with wide eyes peering from my pallid face I opened my mouth to speak, but my trembling bottom lip rendered me speechless.

'Oh, don't start that again. Get a grip.'

'I'm scared.' I managed in a high pitched squeak.

'You're always scared. It's about time you conquered your nerves; carry on like this and you'll be in trouble.'

'Come with me please,' I begged. 'I'll be all right if you're there.'

'I can't. I've things to do. Besides, you have to start going it alone.'

'But I'm frightened Jess.'

'Frightened of what? There's nothing can harm you.'

'There might be something in there.'

'Well, if there is you know what to do. I've shown you enough times.'

'Please, just come to the door with me. We always used to do everything together.'

'Yes, but things are different now. You have to prove you can cope alone.'

'Just to the door, please.' I knew from experience he'd relent. Together we moved towards the house, my hand clinging desperately to Jess's arm.

'Will you calm down?' Jess's voice echoed eerily in the raging silence.

'The house looks spooky Jess. I don't like it. Those windows, they look like eyes on fire.'

'It's only the setting sun's reflection."

"And that big wooden door. It looks threatening. Ready to suck me in and never let me go.'

'Oh God, your imagination. It's just a door, just a house. You've got to stop all this or you'll be the laughing stock when we get back. Right, here's the door, I refuse to go any further.'

'Just stay with me a bit longer,' I pleaded.

An exasperated Jess pushed open the door. It creaked loudly, rooting me to the spot as I let out a terrified little squeal.

'In.' Jess pushed me roughly into the dark, dusty hallway but was unable to disengage himself from my grip. We stood in the hall waiting for our eyes to adjust to the dinginess. I wanted to run, but there was no escape.

Jess opened the door into the lounge. Darkness had taken over now, the last of the sun's rays replaced by moonlight. The atmosphere was cold, musty and uninviting; I felt goose bumps erupt. The silvery shards of light illuminated the outlines of the furniture within the room. My stomach knotted, my breathing escalated as fresh waves of panic rippled through me.

Jess wandered over to a cupboard and returned clutching a bottle and two glasses. He held the bottle up to the shaft of light as he read the label.

'Jack Daniels. Good taste. Here, this will calm your nerves. He handed me a glass containing a generous helping of the amber liquid.

'But we're not allowed,' I protested weakly.

'Who's to know? Get it down you.'

I took a swig of the drink and felt calmer almost immediately. We sat for a long time, talking and refilling our glasses. I definitely felt much braver and rather sleepy too.

I woke with a start, to the sound of approaching footsteps and strange voices.

'Jess,' I hissed. 'I can hear something. What shall I do?'

'You know what to do,' Jess yawned and stretched. 'Get this haunting under your belt and you'll be a fully qualified ghost. You can do it, have faith. '

I knew he was right. In life I had always been terrified of poltergeists and the supernatural. If I had known that Jess and I would drown as a result of a boating accident then maybe it would have been wiser to be frightened of water. Actually becoming a ghost had not cured my phobia and I'd been constantly mocked by my companions in the spirit world. With the help of Jess and the whisky I knew the time had come for me to prove my worthiness and carry out my first solo haunting.

'Okay, I'm going to do it. Lay the ghost, as they say.' I managed a smile as I braced myself.

'Good lad, that's the spirit.' Jess's laughter hung in the air as he faded away.

Over The Top

I'm in the garden killing a cabbage. One of the things I love about gardening is the opportunity to vent frustrations and behave violently without involving the law. Mind you, right now I'm rapidly beginning to wonder if I should call the police to search for my wife who's been missing since this morning. Where the hell is she?

The slaughtered cabbage is dark green, crisp and pungent. Ideal accompaniment for a roast dinner should anyone be available to prepare it. My stomach and the fridge are empty and much as I love to grow edible produce, I have no idea how to cook it and no inclination to learn. That's her department, or at least it was until recently.

In theory retiring to the coast seemed a good move and I hoped it would give her a new lease of life. The temperate climate and rich soil are ideal for my horticultural passion and I secretly nursed the idea she'd become interested and involved. Experience should have warned me there'd be as much chance of that as world peace, but I'm ever the optimist. If I caved in to reality life would be unbearable apart from my garden. A rare haven for sensory delight and inner peace. In truth I have more affection for the carrots I've just pulled than my wife.

Serves me right really for rushing things. I should have looked around for a more compatible partner instead of getting hitched to the first woman who showed an interest. Ours wasn't a marriage made in heaven, more in error. But things were tolerable while she stuck to her side of the bargain, leaving me to mine. Her life of domestics, soaps and trivia hardly makes for an exciting partner, but at least it ensured my dinner was on the table, my socks in pairs and conversation kept to a minimum. But now, after all these years she's started behaving strangely and I can't figure out why.

It's almost dark when I hear the click of her key in the lock. She bursts into the lounge smiling like a demented clown, wearing an expression I'd only associate with a teenager high on crack, a lottery winner or post coital ecstasy. I know none of those are the reason for her smug countenance as she's too cautious to indulge in anything mood altering, too frugal to purchase a lottery ticket and too damned ugly to attract any admirers. She's a dumpy woman with thin lips and thick glasses.

'Where on earth have you been until this time? I'm starving and you've not done any shopping.' Not the most subtle approach I know, but I'm weary of her recent furtiveness.

'Oh don't start, Gerald. You and your stomach. What do you care anyway?'

Hostility and the distinct odour of stale sweat linger in the air. She's obviously been exerting herself in some way, which is totally out of character. She generally has the vitality and intellect of a geriatric slug.

'You could have phoned. I was worried about you, ' I lie.

'That would be a first. Anyway, my phone's dead. It needs recharging.'

'Why? You hardly ever use it.'

'Well I do now.'

'What's going on with you? You're out all hours, nothing gets done at home and now it seems you're always on the phone.'

She hesitates, then sighs, averting her narrow eyes. 'If you really want to know I've started geocaching.'

'Geo what?'

'I'm too tired to explain and I doubt you'd be interested anyway. Look it up on the internet if you really want to know.

I'm going to bed. ' Her face resumes its agitated, squinty look. I guess I burst her bubble and will be penalised for it tomorrow.

The door slams and I'm reduced to making a sandwich. Later I can't resist the temptation of checking out what it is that's distracting my wife from her duties. Turns out this geocaching business has been going on for years. It's some sort of treasure hunting game where you use a GPS to search for containers hidden all over the world. When you find one you have to sign a logbook inside the container then log it on the website later. Well, Whoopdedo. What a bloody waste of time.

Things deteriorate over the next few weeks. I'm forced to spend more time harvesting salad crops as the wife's rarely available to cook. Weight is dropping off me without any decent meals and my unwashed clothes are too large. The dirty house is in chaos and I'm rapidly reaching the end of my rope. I know I wanted her to develop an interest in something, but this geocaching racket has turned into an obsession. Completely over the top.

Today she even threatened to have the garden slabbed if I don't stop complaining. In order to pacify her I've had to agree to take her out in the car tonight to find one of the blessed caches. She had to give up driving a few years ago when her myopia took a turn for the worse. Turns out this geocache can only be hunted out in darkness as it's reflective and can't be seen in daylight. I've not seen her this excited since the last time I bought her a new cooker. Maybe she'll even use it once she's logged her latest find.

'It's up on the downs near that monument. I reckon it's hidden in a tree stump,' she relays enthusiastically as I drive with gritted teeth and a rumbling belly. 'You can walk behind me and read the instructions while I use the map on my phone.' I've never felt so underwhelmed.

I park the car and she heads out into the darkness with her flashlight and phone. There's a hint of autumn in the air and I button my coat against the chill wind. I trail behind her praying she'll locate the stupid geocache quickly so we can get home for some dinner.

'How many metres north of the monument is it? ' Her voice echoes in the misty, evening air. 'I can't see the phone very well. Just check the instructions will you? Is it twenty?'

I hold my torch over the paper. A thought pops into my head. It's pure evil, but my mouth takes control before I can stop it. 'No, it's thirty metres.'

It's quiet for a few minutes then her voice again, fainter, more indistinct. 'Are you sure? I thought…'

A screech fills the air, reminiscent of a cat on helium, followed by a distant thud and then silence.

By the time an ambulance arrives the tide has come in and the body been washed away from the rocky beach where she fell from the cliff's edge. An attractive female police officer drives me home in my car as she's concerned I might be too shocked and upset after such an awful accident. I'm reduced to making a sandwich again.

A few weeks later the same police officer drops by to inform me they're calling off the hunt for my wife's body as the seas are rough at this time of year and there's little hope of discovering it now. We get chatting over tea and fig rolls and she tells me she understands how devastated I feel as she lost her husband a couple of years ago. She confides she's about to retire from the police service and is contemplating securing an allotment to work on during her free time.

'Tell you what,' she says. "I can see you're not looking after yourself too well, so how about we go and dig up some of those beautiful home grown vegetables out there and I'll rustle you up a decent meal.

Bingo. A good looking widow with twenty-twenty vision, plus a love of gardening and cooking. If I decide to search for a replacement I'll be a lot more careful this time, but it's looking promising. A step in the right direction if you'll excuse the pun.

Love Thy Neighbour

Jeremy had no ambition. And that was the ultimate sin in the Campbell household. In his home, "Excelsior," there was only one direction to go in life – upwards, and woe betide anyone who did not conform. Jeremy's younger sister Emily was already preparing for a dozen or more *A* grades and a place at Cambridge. His father, being a successful solicitor was enterprising, committed and pushy, Jeremy was nothing like him. His mother was a first class snob and chairperson of every committee in the area; the Hyacinth Bucket of the posh estate where they resided. Jeremy hated both his parents and everything they stood for.

Jeremy sought solace tinkering with the old motorbike he kept in the shed at the bottom of the garden. Out of sight. He'd tried parking it on the extensive drive of their oversized, detached house but Mother soon put a stop to that.

'A motor bike. Really Jeremy, what would the neighbours think? Why can't you get a nice little sports car like your father?'

But Jeremy had dug his heels in; as he always did. He had a passion for all things mechanical, his only aim in life to be a motor mechanic.

'A motor mechanic. Really Jeremy, what would the neighbours think?' was Mother's predictable reply when he had dared mention it. 'You'll stay at school, obtain some qualifications; get a good job like your father.'

Jeremy had no intention of staying on at school and silently made plans to take up a motor mechanic's apprenticeship as soon as school finished this summer. He would leave this clinical, loveless place supposedly called home and move in with his girlfriend Lorna and her mother.

They had no idea he still saw Lorna; bunking off school to meet her in town every day. Jeremy remembered the one night he had risked bringing her home to meet his family.

'Don't think you're taking up with that common little madam,' his mother stated coldly the minute Lorna had left. 'Everyone knows she lives with her unmarried mother on that filthy council estate, sponging off decent people like us. It's disgusting. And don't even think about bringing her here again. Really Jeremy, what would the neighbours think?'

Two weeks later Jeremy waved goodbye to his parents and sister as they set off for a three-week Mediterranean cruise. He'd cried off going with them on the grounds that he needed to study, intending to carry out his plan the minute they had gone.

'Look after the house and garden,' his mother reminded him. 'And behave yourself. We don't want the neighbours complaining when we get back.'

Jeremy packed quickly then thought maybe he had better take some means of identification with him if he intended to start his new life. He spent ages in his parent's bedroom searching for the sort of box that would typically hold family documents. His mother had ensured it was well hidden.

Jeremy opened the box. The first shock came when he discovered his parent's marriage certificate. Jeremy may not have passed any maths exams, but it didn't take him long to work out that the marriage had taken place two years after he was born.

At the bottom of the box, he found what he was looking for. Jeremy opened the birth certificate, his face registering confusion then astonishment as he studied the entry in scripted hand in the space designated "Name of father." Jeremy checked it for the fourth time, making sure he'd read it correctly. "Thomas Jones – occupation, motor mechanic." Well, well, well.

When the shock had subsided, Jeremy felt a strange sense of relief in the knowledge that he was no relation to the man he had called Father all his life. He decided his passport would be sufficient means for identification purposes. He threw it into his bag and fastened the zip.

Jeremy straddled his motorbike, raised two fingers then roared off towards the two-up two-down semi on the council estate where he knew he would find warmth, love and happiness. He smiled as he imagined his mother's face when she saw the offending birth certificate pinned to the front door with his note which simply stated:

"Really mother, what would the neighbours think?"

Merry Widows

'So, tell me all about Rosemary.'

I can see he's impressed; he can't take his eyes off her.

'Well, she's one of a family of around two hundred and originates from Chile. She's about five-years-old and quite a bit bigger than average.'

'She certainly *is* a fine specimen. Her colouring and markings are very distinctive. Is she easy to handle?'

'Oh, Rosemary's very docile, I've looked after her since she was born and there's not a thing I don't know about her.'

'She really is a beauty. Best I've seen all week.'

I reach into the terrarium and proudly stroke her abdomen. Hard to believe how naturally it comes to me after all those years of being a phobic.

'She's been reared in the finest surroundings and fed only the best crickets. I've spent a long time studying the Theraphosidae family and without sounding arrogant, I know my stuff.'

'Where did you study?'

I smile and begin my well rehearsed reply; he doesn't need to know everything. The truth is I became an expert on spiders during the time I spent inside, at Her Majesty's pleasure. In fact, being in jail was probably the best thing that ever happened to me in a perverse sort of way and it certainly cured my phobia.

Through regressive hypnotherapy I learnt my father was to blame. I had a very dull, frugal upbringing; reared on the by-products of milk and never allowed to explore much in the outside world. My father was a Reverend with some *very* weird beliefs, to say the least. He insisted that keeping spiders in the house prevented gout and deliberately brought in the largest, hairiest ones he could find. Childhood ailments were treated with spider dung and urine, my obvious distress and repulsion dismissed as immature tantrums. Regression stirred long-buried memories that explained my overwhelming arachnophobia. Like the day my father went berserk because I left a stain on the best rug in the house.

'Patience, where are you?' he yelled as he stalked through the front door.

Cowering in the corner I managed a whispered 'Here.'

'What's the matter with you girl, and where's my dinner? I come home from church to find you idling on the floor and …what's *that*?' His steely grey eyes bulged from his beetroot-red face as he pointed a rigid finger at the mess on the rug.

'Please don't yell Daddy. I was eating my supper when a massive spider climbed onto my stool. It frightened me and I dropped my bowl when I screamed. Don't be angry daddy, I hate these spiders. Why do we have to keep them?'

My father's answer to that was to lock me in the cellar for a week, ensuring I had the minimum of sustenance and the maximum of gross arachnids for company. I never dare mention my feelings after that, but my phobia intensified by the day.

At sixteen I married the first man prepared to protect me from anything on eight legs. My father conducted the wedding and I'm convinced he was secretly glad to see the back of me. Probably turned my room into a spider sanctuary as soon as I moved out; I've never seen him since.

The marriage wasn't perfect by a long way, but at least there was always someone around to dispose of any unwelcome creepy crawlies. Until that disastrous September night, that is.

We'd been to a friend's birthday party and arrived home in the early hours completely rat-arsed. Hubby fell into a coma almost immediately, but just as I was dozing off I noticed something in the half light scuttling across my pillow. Alcohol had done nothing to dampen my paranoia, but no amount of poking, thumping and pleading could wake my partner from his stupor. Fighting paralysis, I slipped from the bed and returned with the largest frying pan in my kitchen. I'll never forget the sound as I crashed it down on the intended enemy, but even in my inebriated state I realised no spider could bleed that profusely.

The jury was lenient and the prison staff most understanding. Appreciating I was no vicious murderer they put me through a desensitisation programme to help overcome my arachnophobia. Pictures and books to start with, then videos and films, followed by plastic replicas until at last I was ready to face the real thing.

If my father had explained to me the fascinating facts about spiders I don't think I'd have developed the phobia in the first place. The more I learnt, the more I came to respect these canny creatures, eventually becoming totally absorbed. Any species that's survived over three hundred million years deserves admiration.

So, as I served my sentence, the staff encouraged and helped me to become an expert. Starting with the common garden spider I studied their anatomy, habits, moulting, feeding, web construction and mating. The day I watched my first five hundred spiderlings ballooning away from the prison yard was the day I realised I'd become addicted to spiders.

Over the years I've studied and bred hundreds of different species, come to love them all for their unique ways and intriguing behaviour. The staff presented me with my beautiful "Grammostola Cala" tarantula, Rosemary, on my release and even helped fund this trip.

'And is she a good breeder?' The voice interrupts my thoughts.

'Oh yes, in fact I've just returned her last brood to the Chilean Preservation Society. They were all perfect specimens.'

'And the father?'

'Erm, to be honest we didn't rescue him from the terrarium fast enough after the mating. Rosemary made a meal of him so to speak, but to be fair he wouldn't have lived much longer anyway. The males die shortly after breeding, whereas Rosemary here could live another twelve years.'

'Well, I think we need look no further. Welcome to Hollywood Mrs…?'

He offers a hand of congratulation, his eyes settling on my wedding ring.

'Sadly, like Rosemary, I'm a widow and have reverted to my maiden name, Ms Muffet, but you can call me Patience.'

So now Rosemary's landed the starring role in the remake of "Arachnophobia'" and I shall devote my life to the conservation of spiders.

Safe As Houses

I'm not really in the mood for another argument with Vera's gate this morning but it's obviously in fine fighting mode. Hanging precariously to one hinge, it considers my attempt to gain access a signal to behave in an unpredictable, eccentric fashion.

Vera's bungalow stands, or rather slumps like an outcast hunchback, on a huge, neglected plot of land, which could be the envy of the entire neighbourhood. But Vera hasn't the time, inclination or generosity to spend on it so it has become an overgrown wilderness, devoid of colour and structure. The bungalow has suffered the same disregard, time and lack of care, causing it to stare sadly out onto the street through the misty, condensation of its single-glazed windows. Grubby, mismatched curtains hang limply; all bargains from charity shops and all ill-fitting. Most of the time they remain closed. Only the contents of the conservatory are visible from the street, causing passers-by to tut with disgust or gaze in fascination. Cardboard boxes, crates, piles of newspapers and plastic carrier bags containing goodness knows what clutter the floor, leaning haphazardly against the dirt strewn glass. Overlooked plants in cracked pots strain towards what little light there is and silently gasp for water.

Eventually I win my battle with the gate and make my way up the lichen-covered pathway towards the peeling, faded front door. The doorbell doesn't work. Knocking on the door rarely brings a response, but today I am rewarded by the sound of soft shuffling and loud cursing from within. I wait, my pasted smile balancing as unsteadily as the gate, while Vera

70

checks out her visitor through the one-way spy hole, then unleashes numerous bolts and chains. Does she really believe that anyone would actually want to enter this hazard area she calls home unless they have to? As the unaligned door finally opens with an unwelcome creak I am presented with the sight of the hallway from hell and Vera herself; a vision from the worst episode of "What not to Wear." Today she sports an ankle length floral skirt, matched imperfectly with a blue spotted blouse, a yellow striped cardigan, pink fluffy slippers and a scowl.

'Morning Vera. When are you going to get this doorbell fixed?'

'Oh it's you,' she grunts, as if she'd been expecting something better. 'I keep telling you I'll get Stan to do it.'

'You want me to give him a ring while I'm here?'

'No. Do you know how much it costs to make a phone call in the daytime? I'll wait until I bump into him.' I raise my eyes to the patchy, cracked ceiling in exasperation. Sometimes I wonder why I bother.

'I don't know why you don't get a professional to do it Vera. Stan might be cheap and cheerful but he's hardly qualified.'

'Aye well, I've always had Stan do my odd jobs. You can't trust folk these days. And if he can't do it then he'll know a man who can.'

'Or a cowboy,' I reply with restrained cynicism. 'You should spend some money on this place. God knows, you must have thousands in the bank. Get some registered companies who know what they're doing to sort things out. It's a flaming health hazard is this.' Vera goes all tight-lipped and Lady Macbeth as she always does at the mere mention of spending money.

'Anyway, are you coming in or what? I'm freezing to death standing here.'

'Well, you could put the heating on,' I suggest. It falls on deaf ears.

We pick our way round the clutter of tables, chests of drawers, bureaus, books, newspapers and plastic carrier bags, the contents of which I daren't guess, that line both sides of a narrow hallway. I arrive at her lounge door with three fresh bruises and a bout of claustrophobia.

My husband thinks I'm an idiot for trying to help Vera out, but I haven't the heart to cut her off as others have done. She was here when we moved in twenty-odd years ago and I can't ignore the good neighbour instincts my mother instilled in me as a child. Vera's mother didn't do her many favours when she was alive. A large, childless lady in her mid-forties, she was admitted to hospital with a suspected appendicitis and left three days later with a scrawny, wrinkled bundle she later named Vera. The father died shortly after, probably from the shock. Mother passed on several years ago leaving Vera the bungalow, a lifetime's collection of useless clobber and the same reluctance to part with anything.

Vera wastes nothing but time. She spends her days rummaging around charity shops and car boot sales, returning home clutching her newly acquired treasures as if they were the crown jewels. Every available space in her bungalow is cluttered with other people's cast offs; useless paraphernalia she neither uses nor needs. Often, she doesn't even bother unpacking her purchases; hence the countless number of plastic carrier bags littering every room.

The only uncluttered things in her life are her bills; laughably small and yet Vera complains loudly that her rates and taxes are solely responsible for the upkeep of all single mothers, schools, prisons and local amenities. I can't say I care for Vera in an emotional sense; I just feel that at her age someone needs to care for her. A spinster with no family, retired, with no friends, Stan and I are the only company she has. Local children think she's a witch and other neighbours consider her a cantankerous old bat. The latter at least is perfectly true, but my conscience will not allow me to stop coming round every day to check on her, help her out a bit. I've no idea exactly how old she is; Vera gives nothing away, not even her age. But she's getting on now and needs assistance. She'd never be willing to admit or pay for it. Anyway, she'd never trust strangers.

Vera huffs and puffs into the lounge, inaptly named considering there is not an inch of space to lounge in.

'Your fire's low, Vera. Shall I put some more coal on? '

'Just a small piece then. I can't afford more fuel bills this side of Christmas.'

'Come off it, Vera. You must have more money than Tommy Lipton has tea leaves. I've never known you spend anything but a penny.' That reminds me I must clean her bathroom before I leave, if I can fight my way into it. 'Want a cup of tea?'

'Aye why not? There's a teabag by the sink; it's only been used twice.'

I struggle past more obstacles to reach her kitchen and fill the antiquated, rusty kettle she insists on using. There are five more kettles on top of the cupboards, one of them brand new she won in a competition, but Vera is adamant this one boils faster and is therefore more economical.

I clear a tiny space on the kitchen worktop to make her tea. I cram the three out-of-date loaves of bread she purchased from the last minute bargain basket at the local supermarket into her overstuffed freezer compartment. I rearrange the latest piles of hotchpotch crockery she has haggled for and discover the fish and chips I brought round last night left half eaten in their newspaper wrapping. (It saves on washing up liquid).

'You didn't eat all your tea last night then,' I shout from the kitchen. 'Shall I put it out for the birds?'

'No, it'll do for later. I'll warm it up in the microwave.' The only piece of modern technology Vera possesses is the microwave she won in another competition. The sheer speed at which it completes its task is enough to convince Vera that it conserves electricity. I tread carefully around the grass strimmer, garden chair, paint pots, tools and plastic carrier bags with their secret contents that dominate the kitchen floor and present Vera with her tea.

'Can you hang my washing out before you go?'

'I suppose so, but it'd be much easier if you invested in a washing machine and tumble drier you know. And don't tell me you can't afford it.'

Eventually, I locate the bag of pegs and step out into the back garden with a bowl of dripping wet odds and sods washed earlier by Vera in the kitchen sink. Despite being familiar with the many obstructions and hazards of her plot I stumble a few times on uneven paving slabs and debris left by handyman Stan. Cursing, I manage to reach the washing line. The rusty metal pole it's attached to wobbles unsteadily, like a drunken teenager, as I peg out the clothes. Another of Stan's botch jobs.

'Right, I'm off then. I'll pop round tonight and put your bin out for the dustmen.'

'Oh don't bother, there's nothing in it anyway.' No surprises there.

Returning to my own house I pour a large glass of wine and relax in front of the television for a few hours. The upside of paying Vera a visit is that it fools me into believing my own home is immaculate and no housework needs doing urgently.

Later, I put some of our excess garden waste into Vera's bin, wheel it to the front of the property and check, unnecessarily, that her doors are locked. I notice the wind has whipped another piece of loose fencing from her already sparse surrounds. I must have another go at her tomorrow about hiring proper workmen; make her see that even the small amount Stan charges is squandered if it's not a job well done Wisdom is the one thing Vera has failed to acquire for all her many years on earth.

My sleep is interrupted by the sound of sirens, distantly at first but quickly altering to ear-splitting closeness. A bleary-eyed glimpse through the curtains reveals two fire engines parked directly outside. Slipping into my dressing gown I join the expanding group of neighbours staring in open-mouthed horror at the blazing inferno that was Vera's bungalow. Firemen battle furiously to control the flames leaping as high as the eye can see into the night sky, but it is obvious that nothing, including Vera, will be rescued. Despite the shock I cannot suppress the thought that Vera would have been delighted to be spared the cost of a cremation. Neither can I dismiss the relief I feel that I will be spared the mind-boggling task of clearing out her bungalow; something I had always anticipated with dread.

Investigation confirms that the electrician Stan employed to re-wire Vera's home a few weeks ago had about as much knowledge of electronics as Mickey Mouse. The faulty wiring is determined as the cause of the fire that claimed Vera's life, but accidental death is written on the certificate. Suicide caused by her habitual stinginess would be more appropriate.

A few weeks later Stan and I sit in the solicitor's office for the reading of Vera's will.

'To Stan, my faithful handyman,' the solicitor drones, 'I leave my bungalow and furnishings in recognition of all the work he has done for me.'

Stan may have lost the bungalow, but the land is still in tact. I can see his eyes light up and read his mind as he mentally visualises the new property he and his amateur D-I-Y companions will erect on the site. Now would definitely be the time for us to move to a new area if only we could afford it.

'To Maggie, my neighbour, who never believed I appreciated her,' the solicitor continues, 'I leave all my savings.'

Oh wow! Maybe God does move in mysterious ways after all.

The solicitor clears his throat and lowers his eyes before reading on. 'I never did trust them banks Maggie, so you'll find all my money in the plastic carrier bags I keep under my bed. And don't waste it.'

Nice one Vera. Serves me right I suppose for all the times I said you couldn't take it with you.

Ceiling Wax

'Morning Ida,' said Carolyn sleepily to the arachnid that inhabited the far left hand corner of her bedroom ceiling. The room really did need a lick of paint. She'd been dreaming about *him* again and even though now fully awake her thoughts dwelled on the wonderful things they had done together. In truth, Ida the spider probably had more excitement in life than she did, but Carolyn's dreams were something else. Dreams that were not confined to her sleep, but occupied most of her waking thoughts. Slowly, Carolyn realised today was the day. Maybe this time her dreams would become reality.

'Going somewhere nice?' asked the pretty blonde as she applied hot wax to Carolyn's eyebrows, legs and bikini line.

'Just a party,' replied Carolyn lying back and admiring the pristine white ceiling of the local beauty salon. Just a party. Who was she kidding? This was the party she had been waiting for. She had first seen *him* at Alison's party many months ago. Tall, dark and handsome, with sparkling brown eyes and a small scar above his mouth that only added to the magnetism of his smile. She'd dreamed about him day and night ever since then. Carolyn hoped spending the whole morning and half her wages on beauty treatments would ensure success when she met him again tonight at the party.

Carolyn lay back in the bubbly bath and stared dreamily at the bathroom ceiling. Thinking of *him*. She didn't know his name, where he lived or what he did for a living but she hoped she would soon find out. The afternoon spent pampering herself was going to plan. She would look so stunning after all the effort, he'd be unable to resist her. But there was plenty of time, so she gave in to the temptation to lie dreaming in the bath a little longer. She turned on the hot tap to top up the now lukewarm water, but just as she was about to resume her dreaming the inevitable happened - the telephone rang.

After assuring her mother that, yes, she would be careful, and no, she wouldn't drink too much Carolyn replaced the receiver and decided a cup of tea was called for. She sat at the kitchen table envisaging dancing in *his* arms all night followed by a long session of steamy passion. Her fantasy was rudely interrupted by water dripping rapidly through the kitchen ceiling. 'Oh Shit!,'she yelled, taking the stairs two at a time, 'I've left the bloody tap running.'

Carolyn opened her eyes slowly and stared at the ceiling. She'd had the most wonderful dream about *him* and didn't want to leave it. Ida had disappeared. But as she began to focus, she realised this was not *her* bedroom ceiling. Her thoughts began to race. She remembered the flood at her house yesterday and the disappointment she had felt at not being able to go to the party, deciding she would have to clean up and wait for someone to come and check the electrics. Then slowly, a smile spread across her face and she turned to check on the sleeping form next to her. Yes, that scar certainly did enhance his good looks but she had never imagined *him* to be an electrician.

Battle Scars

I never liked me cousin Jimmy even before the war. But because me mam feels sorry for him, I have to write to him every Saturday.

'Poor lad,' she says. 'Stuck out in the middle of nowhere, miles away from his family. Only things he has to look forward to are letters from home.'

Oh yeah? Sounds like he's having a whale of a time to me. Playing football on the moors, messing about in barns and haystacks, paddling in rivers, picking blackberries and riding horses. Even got a trip on a steam train when he was evacuated from London. I've *never* been on one and what is there to do round here now? No cinemas, theatres or football matches since this bloody war started. Only place that's stayed open is the church. It's no fun being stuck at home listening to "Worker's Playtime" and Wilfred Pickles reading the news on the wireless or playing draughts all night. I'd swap places with our Jimmy any day. But me mam says I don't understand.

'It's no life for a young lad in the country,' she says. 'Living with strangers and being looked down on by the locals. They don't take kindly to city folk you know. You should think yourself lucky to be able to stay at home with your family. I bet he's eating his heart out.'

Whatever he's eating it has to be better than what we get: black bread, powdered bloody eggs and milk, potatoes, carrots (Mam says they'll help me see in the blackout) and Spam, Spam, Spam. Jimmy gets proper creamy milk from the cows and fresh eggs straight from a chicken's bum. They grow loads of different fruits and vegetables on the farm; said he had some asparagus last week, whatever that is. *And* he doesn't have to stand in a queue for ages to get it.

The rationing just gets worse by the day. I got in trouble on Monday for giving the last of the sausages to the dog.

'Do you know how long I had to queue to get them?' Mam yelled. 'Just for that, our Raymond, you can go up to Gilbert's with the ration book. I've heard they've got some oranges and bananas in and don't come back without any.'

I was there for *hours* and then me mam wouldn't even let me have an orange. I bet she sent one to our Jimmy.

'You want to be grateful, our Raymond,' she says. 'At least you can go to school with your friends and be comfortable. Poor Jimmy has to walk miles every day to an overcrowded classroom full of strangers.'

I wished there'd been more kids in my class on Tuesday then maybe I wouldn't have got the blame for the gas mask incident. We have to do the bloody drill every day and I hate it. Half an hour sitting there with that stupid Mickey Mouse mask on, smelling of rubber and misting up so you can't see anything. I was so bored I coughed just to see how it would sound and it made a noise just like someone trumping. Of course, every one started laughing and copying and I had to stand in the corner for the rest of the day.

Then on Wednesday me mam caught me outside during the blackout. I'd been sitting at the table under the gas lamps reading me "Beano" when I thought I heard a Lancaster Bomber go over. I'm getting dead good at recognising plane engines and I just wanted to check. I daren't look out the window; you're not allowed to open the blackout curtains and anyway you can hardly see through the glass for the tape we've had to put on to stop them exploding if a bomb goes off. So, I tiptoed across the lino to the kitchen, went into the scullery and out the back door. I'd have got away with it too if I hadn't tripped over the washboard in the back yard. Couldn't see a damned thing and it didn't half hurt. Anyway, it *was* a Lancaster Bomber but my pleasure was short lived.

'Get in here this minute,' me mam hollered. 'Bath and early bed for you, young man. And wait until your father gets home.'

Dad arrived soon after from patrolling with the Home Guard. He wasn't too mad at me to start with.

'Where's the dog?' He asked after he'd finished his tea. ' I don't know; I've not seen him for ages.' Mam searched the house but he was nowhere to be found.

'I reckon he must have slipped out when our Raymond opened the door. You'll have to go and find him Bert; we can't leave him out all night.'

Me dad didn't half curse. You try finding a black dog in the middle of the night when you can't even strike a match or use a torch. Not that our torch works anyway; not since I put the batteries in the stove to try and recharge them a bit. I went upstairs and forgot about them; they melted all over the oven and the pong lasted for days. Me mam made me clean out the fireplaces in all the rooms for a week after that.

Anyway, Dad came back with the dog and brought the tin bath in from the yard.

'Right, you can help me fill the bath.'

'Aw mam, do I have to? Can't I just have a wash in me bedroom basin? There's still some water left in the jug from this morning.'

'No, you can't be trusted. You'll be clean even if you're shabby. I see you've made another hole in your vest. I'll have to undo it and knit it up again. I wish you'd be more careful Raymond, you know we've only got a few clothing vouchers left.'

It took ages to boil the water and fill the tub and then I had to wait until after every one else, by which time the water was getting cold and scummy. They have a proper bathroom in that house where our Jimmy's staying. Still, at least I got a full night's sleep that night, not like Thursday.

It was really cold and I was quite glad in a way that we have to sleep in half our clothes to save time if we have to get up for an air raid. I was just dozing off when the sirens started;

made me jump out me skin and then I kicked the chamber pot over when I got out of bed. Me mam was mad about that too; she made me stay in the pantry on me own for half an hour after the all clear. We don't have a proper Anderson shelter like Jimmy's family in London so we all have to cram in there when there's a threat of an air raid. Then later me dad made me go out with him to help put out the fires caused by incendiary bombs.

'I'll fill the stirrup pump; you fetch the sandbag,' he bawled. I didn't like to tell him I'd used all the sand to make mud pies and replaced it with soil. Good job it was dark or he'd have had me guts for garters.

I've had a rotten week altogether, but at least yesterday our Pam gave me something to gloat about in me letter to Raymond. I've not been very nice to her lately; she seems to be having a much better time than me since the war started. I've lost count of how many boyfriends she's had and they all look the same to me in their uniforms anyway. But on Friday she brought home someone really different; I never thought I'd be grateful to me sister or enjoy writing to me cousin.

"Dear Jimmy,

Our Pam's got a new boyfriend and guess what? He's a Yank! He's dead tall and handsome and he talks just like Clark Gable. He's going to get me mam and dad a gramophone and buy them that Glen Miller record. He gave me some sweets and chocolate and tinned fruit and some chewing gum. It's dead minty and it lasts for ages. I'd send you a piece but me mam says she doesn't want it to get stuck on the lovely knitted vest in the parcel we're sending. I stuck last night's piece on the table leg after I'd finished chewing it. You can have that bit when you come home."

For the first time in ages I'm quite pleased I wasn't evacuated like our Jimmy.

Flights Of Fantasy

'Timothy, are you up yet, your egg's getting cold.'

Tim Templeton turned over in bed and gritted his teeth. God, how he hated his mother. He'd prayed the night before, as he always did, that she would die in her sleep, but the Almighty was either elsewhere or enjoyed watching him suffer.

'Coming,' he grunted, 'And *don't* call me Timothy.'

'It's the name you were christened and that's what I'll call you as long as I live,' came the predictable reply.

'Which won't be much longer if I've got anything to do with it,' muttered Tim as he forced himself from his warm bed.

At least it was Friday, last day at the crisp factory which he hated, payday and the evening that Katrina, the insurance agent visited the house. Drop dead gorgeous that one; just the thought of her made it difficult for him to pull on his greasy jeans. He'd always found it hard to talk to girls and even on Saturdays at the pub, lubricated by alcohol, his chat up lines always failed miserably. But he was sure Katrina really fancied him; the way she looked at him, her smile and her more frequent visits to the house. Maybe tonight he'd pluck up the courage to ask her out. But he had the day to get through yet. Fantasies about Katrina would make shovelling the crisps from the hot fat more tolerable and help him get through.

'About time too,' complained his mother as he stumbled into the kitchen. 'God, you look a sight and will you move this bloody heap of plastic off the draining board.

'It's not a heap of plastic; it's a Hawker Hurricane, so you leave it alone, I put it on there to dry out of the way of your bloody cats; rotten, stinking fleabags.'

'At least my cats are real and serve a purpose,' snapped his mother. "You and your bloody stupid Airfix models cluttering up the house. One day I'll trip over one and break me bloody neck I will.'

'In my dreams,' whispered Tim as he pulled on his coat.

'Timothy, you haven't had your breakfast,' shrieked his mother to his retreating back.

'Tim,' he yelled before slamming the front door.

By the time he reached the crisp factory across town, the walk and the fresh air had calmed him some and cleared his head. But thoughts of disposing of his mother would not go away so easily. He had hated her with venom from way back. He had never known his father; Mother having told him they had married young and he had died tragically in an accident. He often wondered what sort of a man he had been; eventually concluding a pretty desperate one to take up with that woman. Not the most feminine of creatures; unlike Katrina

'Ah, Katrina.' He sighed as he turned over the crisps, bubbling furiously in the fat. Ten years now she'd been coming to the house to collect the money on the life insurance. It didn't matter that she was older; he'd been obsessed with her even as a spotty teenager. Now in his twenties, he knew he'd fallen in love, the lifelong problem with girls he blamed on his mother.

'Morning Tim,' smiled Vic, his only friend at the factory, as he stopped his fork lift truck for a quick chat. 'How's yer mother this morning? Mine's been a pain.'

'Same as usual, moaning and miserable. Be happy enough to take me wages off me tonight though, I'll bet, just to pay for her bloody animals.'

'Aye, about time we got away from all this if you ask me. See you down the pub tomorrow then?'

'Sure. In need of a stiff drink or ten,' replied Tim.

Saturday night out with the lads was his only pleasure these days, apart from making his models, but it usually left him stony broke as his mother had always demanded the bulk of his wages. Christ, to be rid of her. No more moaning, money in his pocket and free to ask Katrina to move into what would then be his animal free home.

Life with Katrina occupied his thoughts for the day until he hurried home in anticipation of seeing her in the flesh, the woman of which dreams are made.

'Timothy, is that you?' Mother screeched before he'd even set foot through the door. 'Put the kettle on; make us a cuppa, no sugar for Katrina remember.'

'Hello Tim,' smiled Katrina warmly as he entered the room carrying the tray of tea and biscuits. 'I was just telling your mother that her life policy has matured now. Good news for you isn't it, Muriel?'

'Aye, be alright if I drop off me perch, you will Timothy,' she sneered begrudgingly 'And move this bloody plane thingy off the coffee table. Flaming models.'

'It's not a plane thingy, it's a Westland Whirlwind Helicopter and you keep your mitts off it, I live here too you know.' Tim handed over his wage packet. 'God knows I pay enough for the pleasure; I'll deserve that payout when you pop your clogs, it's been paid for out *my* money.'

'Ungrateful bugger.' Muriel turned to Katrina, 'Always done me best for him, he knows I've never been able to work. Giving birth to him damaged me permanently you know, but I've suffered in silence all these years. Given him everything and what do I get in return?'

'A pine coffin preferably.' Tim, out of earshot, climbed the stairs to his bedroom to work on his Lancaster Bomber, his biggest and best model yet.

'Well, did you ask her out?' enquired Vic the following evening as he passed the refilled pint pots around the table unsteadily. The lads had been at the "Cat and Parrot" public house since eight and were nudging the state known as paralytic.

'No, never got the bloody chance with me mother hovering round all the time. Tell you what though; the old bag's life insurance policy has matured. If I could just find a way of bumping her off I'd be made. No more crisp factory, house to myself and Katrina in me bed. It's tempting I can tell you.'

'Aye, maybe it's worth a serious thought or two," agreed Vic. 'Come round to my place tomorrow and we'll talk it through. Oh, and bring your Messerschmitt; not seen that one yet.'

But Tim didn't make it to Vic's house on Sunday. The police concluded that he had tripped on his Lancaster Bomber, carelessly left on the stairs, when he'd staggered drunkenly to bed the previous night. Accidental death.

'Oh my God,' Muriel had sobbed. 'I was always telling him not to leave the damn models lying about everywhere. And now he's gone.' She had appeared inconsolable.

After the police had left, Muriel poured herself a large brandy. Still trembling she slumped into the chair. Her mind went back to the past. Pregnant at sixteen and dumped by the bastard who put her in the club, she developed a severe hatred of men. She'd resented Timothy from the day he was born and set out from the start to make his life as miserable as her own. With no intention of working she had feigned illness and devoted herself to her many and varied pets.

Timothy was a thorn in her flesh. A failure at school and hopeless with girls he had taken to making Airfix models as a substitute for sex. A no hoper, he had ended up in a dead end job at the crisp factory, his meagre income only just enough to keep her animals and pay for the life insurance. His, not hers.

But then, ten years ago, Katrina had walked into her life and Muriel had realised at that moment exactly why she had such an aversion to men. They had wanted to set up together right from the start; only lack of funds and her bastard son stood in their way. They had planned it together and it looked

85

like they'd pulled it off. She knew those models would come in useful one day; she'd planted the plastic aeroplane on the stairs knowing Timothy would come home legless that night.

Smiling smugly, Muriel picked up the phone and dialled.

'Katrina, my sweet. It worked. It's all over. Pack your case and bring over a bottle of plonk. Monday morning we cash in that policy and take the first flight to somewhere exotic. Oh, and will you pick up a few boxes of Whiskas? The neighbours will see to the cats. Love you.'

Bridging The Gap

My days always start the same way. I leave the house in plenty of time to go through my pre-school rituals. This morning it's raining. Damn. I hate having to hang about in weather like this but needs must. After turning the corner I slip into a quiet alleyway. I turn over the waistband of my skirt four times so the hem just reaches mid-thigh. Slipping off the black sensible lace ups I hate, I reach into my bag and bring out the trainers I secretly saved up for with my pocket money. Once they are on my feet, I slip off my school tie, undo my shirt collar and unravel the plaits in my hair. Now I look like the rest of the girls. Shaking loose my long, black mane I continue my journey to school.

'Morning Pippa,' my best friend Leanne greets me at the school gates. 'Like my new nail varnish?' She flashes her immaculate crimson nails in my direction. Nail varnish. I should be so lucky. They'd never let me wear that.

'No, Philippa,' is always the answer when I ask for make-up or cosmetics. 'You're pretty enough as you are and besides you're much too young.' But I'm thirteen for God's sake. Then they drone on about lipstick and war paint being for women of the night, whatever they are. It's just not fair; all my friends wear it. Why can't they realise I'm almost grown up now?

It wasn't so bad when I was a kid; I never really noticed how different they were to other parents or how different they'd made me. Not having any friends at school didn't bother me either; I was quite content to play solitary games in the only home I'd ever known. But things have changed. Don't get me wrong; I know they love me and I love them, but now

I realise they've wrapped me up in cotton wool all my life like a porcelain doll. Mollycoddled me like a pet poodle and now I want to slip the collar and make a run for it. I was about eleven when it dawned on me.

I got a break when we moved to a new area and I started at the local Comp. I have to be devious and I feel a bit guilty about that, but so far I've been accepted as one of the gang and I'm doing my best to keep it that way. I'm sure they'd all make fun of me if they knew about my home situation so I'm determined they'll never find out.

We tumble into our registration group laughing and joking. Most times I don't understand what they snigger about, but I know it's something to do with sex. That's not a word that exists in my house, so I have to pretend I understand their jokes. As long as I laugh loudly enough no one questions me so it's okay.

'Good morning Mrs Wright, good morning everyone,' we chant as our form teacher embarks on the register.

'Before you go to assembly I have something to tell you. The Friday we break up for Christmas we're holding an Eighties night to raise money for the school. I want you to come along with your parents and join in. It will give you a chance to criticise their music and laugh at their antics on the dance floor for a change. Make sure you take a letter home tonight and ask your parents to fill in the order form for tickets. I expect you all to support the occasion.'

Oh my God, my worst nightmare.

'Sounds like a laugh,' Leanne says as we jostle towards the hall. 'Be nice for our parents to meet. I bet they'd get along just as well as we do. See you later.'

The thing is I don't have any parents. I don't remember anything about the road accident that claimed their lives and unfortunately, or maybe fortunately, I don't remember them either. So, I've never missed them; home is my grand parent's house and it's all I can relate to. But now, I really miss the *idea* of them; a youngish couple who I could take along to the dance, who would allow me some teenage freedom and understanding. My grandparents do their best I know, but they're just so, well, so *old*. I mean, they must be well over fifty and that's just ancient. Their record collection is pure vinyl, they think a text message is something from the Bible and the World Wide Web has something to do with the conservation of spiders. I've had to learn about computers at our local Cyber cafe, catch up on pop music in record stores and phone my friends on an antiquated mobile I purchased on e-bay. I manage to keep up with my friends, but it's hard work and I know my teenage experiences are lacking by comparison. It would just be so embarrassing if they found out I live with a couple of dinosaurs.

I've avoided taking friends home; I've adopted my own ingenious methods of coping with peer pressure, but this one is really going to be a bummer. How could I take my grandparents to an Eighties night? I doubt they can even remember how to jive let alone dance along to Duran Duran, and they're certainly in no condition to attempt it. If only I had some aunts and uncles I could borrow for the night but sadly, I'm an only child and so were my parents.

Walking home from school that evening, pondering the problem, the rain comes on even heavier and I dive into a phone booth to restore my schoolgirl image instead of using the usual alleyway. Skirt lengthened, sensible shoes replaced and plaits restored I look in the tiny mirror to check my reflection and notice a pink card pinned to the notice board.

"Tanya and Ross. Swinging couple seek flexible girl for fun nights."

Have my prayers been answered? Maybe Tanya and Ross have been heaven sent to act as my parents for the dance. Well, I can be fun and I know for a fact I'm flexible. My P.E. teacher says I have a spine like a rubber band. I dial the number and make an appointment to meet them. Tanya sounds really nice.

Their address is on my route home, so I put on my best little girl lost expression and nervously press their doorbell, then smile sweetly at the pretty blonde who opens the door.

'Hi, I'm Pippa. I rang about your advert.'

Tanya looks me up and down with an expression I've never come across before.

'Ross,' she shouts. 'You better come down.'

They're a nice couple and as I sit with a hot cup of tea and a custard cream I tell them my story. It turns out Ross went to school with my dad and remembers my grandparents.

'So you see, when I saw your advert I thought maybe I could hire you to be my parents for the night. How much do you charge? I've a bit of money saved up.' I conclude. They look really trendy and young; I bet they really do swing on the dance floor.

Tanya and Ross look at each other and I can tell they're dying to laugh but as usual I can't see the joke.

'Tell you what,' Tanya smiles. 'You're not quite what we had in mind, but we've got kids of our own and we know how tough it can be. How about we take you home and have a chat with your grandparents. We'll tell them we heard of your circumstances and knowing what a reliable girl you are we'd like you to baby-sit for us sometimes when we go out.'

So now I baby-sit for Tanya and Ross quite a lot. Their kids are great and the extra money helps too. My grandparents really took to them; especially as Ross was a friend of the son they miss so much. They've sort of adopted them and things have worked out really well for us all. Tanya has convinced my grandma that I need to be allowed to grow up and fit in with my friends, so now she takes me shopping every Saturday for clothes and make up. I can see my grandma flinching every time she looks at my crimson talons and four-inch heels but she'll not say anything. The other day I overheard her telling Tanya that I'd been much happier since they came along and that she was sorry she'd forgotten what it was like to be young.

'But, you're not old,' Tanya said to my gran. 'You just need to bring your image up to date.'"

On the day of the dance Tanya took my gran for an overhaul at the beauticians and then they went shopping for new outfits. I hardly recognise her now as she sways on the dance floor. Granddad's not doing too badly either despite his arthritis. Mind you, they're not a patch on Tanya and Ross; they really are the best swingers in the room.

I feel so proud and happy. My friends think my grandparents are cool; some of them never see theirs or haven't even got any. I never looked at it that way before. So, no more secrets, no more rituals and no more pretending.

My grandparents bought me a computer and a new mobile phone for Christmas. Tanya and Ross gave me a stereo system for my bedroom. I go round on Boxing Day to thank them.

'You're welcome love,' they say, hugging me as if I'm their own.

'How are your grandparents?'

'Oh, they're great. They reckon they're the oldest swingers in town thanks to you two.'

They look at each other just as they did that first time we met. I can see they're ready to burst out laughing, but I still don't understand why. Maybe I'm not as grown up as I thought and have a lot to learn yet. But one thing I have learnt is that my friends like me just as I am, with or without parents.

Just A Minute

"It is Monday today. It is cloudy today. Last night I went to the pictures…" wrote number forty-two on the register in her clear, rounded hand. Polly Wilson, the seven-year-old from hell. Or so her family believed. At school it was different. Polly loved school, devoured the challenges, escaped into her fantasy world. But why did every day have to start with writing this rotten diary? Everyone knew what day it was, it was written on the blackboard. Everyone knew what the weather was like, walked to school in it hadn't they? Precious waste of time and pencil lead; not like writing stories.

For Polly, every previous night had been spent at the pictures, more precisely the local cinema where her mum worked as an usherette. Elegant and slim in her green uniform with the golden epaulettes on her bony shoulders, she directed people to their seats with her torch and Polly thought she looked stunning.

They didn't think she understood why they sent her up to the cinema every night to join her mum. Said the exercise would do her good and it would be a change of scene. Or scenes. She didn't mind the films really, got to see them all free of charge and enjoyed the excitement of being allowed to watch the 'A' rated ones. Yes, films helped her to stay safe in her fantasy world. She knew the real reason she was sent out of the way was to give her dad, her grandparents and her bloody sister a tantrum free break. A bit of peace and quiet.

Teachers understand, parents often don't, that children will go to any lengths to gain attention. At school, glowing praise and approval equalled quiet, hard working angel. At home, comparison and criticism equalled brat. And the answer to that was to create a fuss. Little Polly Wilson had perfected the art. She could never write in her diary what really went on. Take this morning.

'Polly,' her mother had snapped loudly. 'Get up. You'll be late. Your sister's been ready for half an hour.'

'Aw mum, just a minute.'

'And stop doing that, you'll go blind. Up!'

Breakfast and ablutions completed the predictable last enquiry ensued.

'Have you been, Polly?' Sulky silence, hanging head, Mother groping her backside.

'Not again you stupid girl. I'm sick and tired of you wetting your knickers. I'll have to start sending you to school in nappies. Why the hell didn't you go?'

'I'm not going in there after *he's* been in, it bloody stinks.' The bog at the end of the yard. Even holding her nose didn't eradicate the invasive mixture of crap, fag smoke and newspaper that filled the cold, damp air.

'Don't be rude about your granddad. God, you are *such* a pain. I sometimes wish I'd never had you, I do. And stop bloody swearing.'

'Aye, just a minute of pleasure and a lifetime of pain that one,' agreed Granddad, sucking a piece of well done toast. He'd left his teeth in the bedroom again.

"It is Tuesday today. It is foggy today. Last night I went to the pictures…" It had been a good one too. Doris Day in "The Pyjama Game." A real fantasy story. It had helped her to forget the teatime incident.

Nobby greens. Polly's worst nightmare. She'd tried to sidle down from the table hoping no one would notice the green balls of poison hidden under the cold mash.

'Just a minute, my girl,' her grandma had yelled. 'You're not leaving that table until you've eaten every one of those sprouts.' What Grandma lacked in stature she certainly made up for in volume.

'I can't eat them, I hate them. I won't,' Polly replied defiantly.

'Then you'll stay there all night and I'll tell your mother when she gets in. She'll give you one. Your sister's eaten all hers. God, I don't know what your mum and dad did to deserve one like you.'

Polly knew what they'd done. She'd seen it in one of those "A" rated films. Strange. Couldn't imagine them doing that, they spent all their time trying to avoid each other.

By seven o' clock they'd had enough of her. Given in. Sent her up to the cinema. But it was no victory; she knew she'd be deprived of her egg and chips on Friday by way of a punishment.

"It is Wednesday today. It is windy today. Last night I went to the pictures…"

Disturbing scenes from "The Invisible Man" still filled Polly's head. Her mother had laughed at it but it had upset Polly. But how she wished she could be invisible sometimes and then it wouldn't have happened. She hadn't slept well last night.

'Polly,' her mother had shouted up the stairs. 'What are you doing now? You're supposed to be brushing your teeth.'

'Just a minute,' Polly replied, trying to sound frothy.

She was sitting on her parent's bed. Taboo. She had crept in, quietly opened the wardrobe door and taken out the giant white Teddy, already christened Timothy, they'd purchased for the approaching Christmas. She was hugging him very close, stroking the soft pristine fur, rubbing her unwashed cheek against his gentle face.

Footsteps on the stairs. No time to hide herself or the bear.

'Polly Wilson, you evil little sod. We knew you'd been doing that. Just can't wait can you? Spoil everything, you do. In that bed now. Santa won't be coming to you my girl, only your sister.'

Santa Claus. Another illusion. Never believed in him anyhow. She knew they'd bought the bear from Nottingham after she'd swooned over it in the shop window.

'What do you want with another teddy bear? Soppy kid, time you grew out of it. Why can't you collect stamps like your sister?'

But they'd bought it. She knew they would. Their fault really, should have hidden it in a more imaginative place.

"It is Thursday today. It is snowing today. Last night I went to the pictures…" Polly had been enraptured by the animated cartoon in glorious Technicolor that had enabled her to temporarily forget the problems of real life. So enraptured in fact, she'd forgotten about the tub of ice cream on her lap until it melted and seeped all over her new skirt. She'd half heartedly wiped it up with her handkerchief but was soon distracted by the wonder of the film. It wasn't until she walked into the parlour at home that the extent of the damage was seized upon by her irate grandmother.

"Polly Wilson, just look at the state of you. What *have* you been doing, you dirty little madam? You don't deserve new clothes. Your sister's cast-offs are too good for the likes of you.'

How could she write in her diary that she'd spent her evening standing on a stool at the scullery sink, attempting to scrub out the stains from her skirt and erase the nagging voices in her head? No supper for her, just a cold bed and a childish longing to be a character in the perfect world of Disney.

It is Friday today. It is raining today. Polly Wilson will not be writing her diary this morning. Registration is taking place in Class Three.

'Thirty nine, forty, forty one …' Silence.

'Polly?" asks Mrs Goldman, lovely warm Mrs Goldman. 'Anyone seen Polly?'

She'd been walking home from school the night before with her friend Jenny, clutching Teddy Robinson who always sat on Mrs Goldman's knee while she read the class story. Knowing there was no egg and chips for tea, not relishing the prospect of going to the pictures. A western. Hated them. All that fighting; she had enough battles in her own life. On impulse she decided to cross the road and visit her Aunty Joan. Didn't look right, look left, look right again.

'Just a minute,' screamed Jenny Too late. The screeching of brakes, a loud thud. The last thing Polly heard was the familiar growl of her teddy bear as it landed in the road beside her now still, bent body.

"It is Monday today. It is sunny today. Last night I went to the pictures…" Polly didn't think the new usherette looked half as glamorous as her mum, but it didn't matter any more. Sitting in the cinema with all her family around her, eating popcorn and watching her favourite film, she'd felt she might just burst with happiness.

It's the beginning of a new term in Mrs Goldman's class and the start of a new life for little Polly Wilson.

The first time Polly's eyes had flicked open from her unconscious state, it had taken just a minute to observe the concern and love in the tear-filled eyes of her family keeping a vigil around her bed. She'd spent a long time in hospital recovering from her accident and things had changed a lot since then. The first night home she'd been unable to sleep and had crept down the stairs for a drink of water. Unable to resist pressing her ear to the living room door, she'd realised she was the topic of conversation being discussed in hushed voices.

'I thought we were going to lose her,' Granddad said in a subdued tone.

'Don't, our Tommy, it doesn't bear thinking about,' Grandma added.

'Well, I think it's time we all pulled together and made an effort for her sake. I'm giving up working nights at the cinema so I can spend more time with her in the evenings. I can always get a job in a shop during the day while she's at school.' Polly resisted the temptation to dash into the room but danced a silent jig behind the closed door as she listened to her mum's plans.

'I'm pleased to hear that,' her dad's voice sounded strangely animated. 'Maybe we can take the girls out more, go on holiday and behave like a proper family.'

There'd been a murmur of agreement and the clink of glasses as the family decided to drink to the future. Polly ascended the stairs two at a time then snuggled down in bed with the new teddy bear her sister had given her when she came home from the hospital. Before drifting into a contented sleep Polly promised herself she'd try to be a good girl; she'd help her mum and grandma, eat her greens and even be nice to her sister.

'Polly, have you finished your diary yet?'

'Just a minute.' Polly gave Mrs Goldman a wide, gap-toothed smile.

There were just so many lovely things she wanted to write in her diary these days.

Walking Disaster

The wheat field stretches ahead as far as the eye can see. Fully ripened heads dance on delicate stalks in the gentle summer breeze, like a thousand golden fingers beckoning. Cotton wool clouds drift lazily across an azure sky; the sun illuminating the dense trees surrounding the field of shimmering grain.

A journey of a thousand miles starts with a single step. As we venture into the field we do not yet realise the irony of those words.

Unsure of what to do with the day, we'd started the morning with a leisurely stroll through Shanklin's old village. Personally, I was hoping it would turn too hot to do anything but laze on the beach but knew from experience Mother would have other ideas. A holiday with my mother is about as relaxing as a fortnight backpacking through Iraq. After the shops, we followed the road to St Blasius church, standing aloof cloaked by ash trees, where we spent some time wandering through the churchyard. At the end of a row of weathered gravestones we'd discovered this unexpected wheat field basking in the summer sunshine.

Mother's studying a signpost. I say goodbye to my lazy afternoon acquiring a sun tan, knowing she'll now have a plan of action forming in her brain.

'Do you fancy a walk to Ventnor?' she asks before I'm quick enough to feign a sprained ankle.

'How far is it?' I reply unenthusiastically.

'I don't know, but it doesn't take long on the bus, does it, so it can't be that far.'

'What about lunch? We haven't brought any sandwiches.'

'Oh, that's typical of you; always thinking of your stomach first. We can have a pub lunch when we get to Ventnor. Come on, it'll do you more good than lolling on a beach.' That's a matter of opinion, but no one else is allowed one.

So begins our journey through the gently undulating field; the dusty aroma of dried earth mingling with the musty scent of wheat ready for harvesting. Our trusty Cairn Terrier, Boo, (don't ask) scampers excitedly ahead of us, camouflaged by the waist-high crops. She's never walked through a field of wheat before. Come to think of it, originating from a city, neither have I. Nor am I aware of the allergy I have to the pollen that floats everywhere around us as we crunch our way towards the woods that lay beyond the field. By the time we reach them I've broken out in a sweaty rash and can't stop sneezing. Do we have any tissues? Of course not. Being summer, sleeves are not an option either. Believe me; wiping a runny, sore nose with sycamore leaves is not a pleasant experience.

Emerging from the woods, we find ourselves confronted by an almost vertical slope stretching into eternity. A monument stands where the summit appears to be, looking like a child's model from this distance. My already struggling lungs wheeze in protest at the thought.

'Oh Mum, I really don't feel like mountaineering in this heat. Shall we turn back?'

'Don't be such a wimp. Where's your spirit of adventure? If I can do it, so can you, just think of the view from the top.' Mother on a mission is unstoppable.

Thirty minutes later, lacking the necessary oxygen to swear or beg for mercy, we collapse onto the monument. The view from here offers two choices. Behind us, the sharp incline we have just tackled; in front, another hill even steeper and longer than the previous one.

'Well, we've come this far,' my over-enthusiastic mother remarks before I can complain. 'I bet we can see the whole island from up there. Come on.' It's at times like this I sometimes wish I'd been orphaned at birth.

Admittedly, the view from the top of St Boniface Down is breathtaking; once we've recovered some breath, that is. In the far distance the horizon meets the English Channel, reflecting the blue of a perfect summer sky, melting into the many rich greens of fields and woodlands caressing the quaint old towns of Shanklin and Ventnor. We pause to rest; sitting on an uneven stone wall to take photographs for the family album.

The climb down is easy by comparison; it's only when we reach the bottom and look back at the stone wall that I realise my expensive camera is still on it. Another climb to retrieve the forgotten camera does nothing to improve my mood or frayed nerves. Exhausted, hungry and thirsty, we ignore the seats placed at regular intervals as we tackle the downward slope again.

'Why is it they always put seats on hills going down?' my mother observes. Logic doesn't run in our family; I ponder again where the genes came from that enabled my sister and I to pass the eleven plus examination. Our father's rarely allowed to speak, so we've never gauged his intelligence level. In fact, we've often contemplated how we even managed to be conceived with parents who come from different planets. Maybe we're adopted, or maybe we just hope we are.

At least now we're on the flat as we continue our walk, following the signpost over a stile and into a grassy field. After a few steps, Mother comes to an abrupt halt.

'What's that over there? They look like cows to me.'

I sense more problems. 'Mother, they're miles away. They can't even see you from that distance. Anyway, they won't hurt you.'

I know it'll fall on deaf ears. My father told her the same thing on a walk along the River Trent a few years ago. After dancing cheek to cheek with an upright Friesian on that occasion, she's never trusted my father or anything bovine since.

'I'm not crossing this field; we'll have to find another route.'

There's no point continuing the discussion. I must admit the distant cows do look rather beefy (excuse the pun) and sinister, with threatening horns and very large dangly bits. (not udders) We turn to leave the field but not before Boo has discovered a juicy cow clap to roll in. Instead of that sunny afternoon on the beach I now have a rash, a blocked nose, blisters, an hysterical mother and a foul-smelling terrier. Oh joy.

The alternative route adds a few extra miles to our trip, as well as nettle stings, insect bites and numerous cuts and grazes from overgrown flora and fauna. The icing on the cake arrives in the form of an unpredicted, torrential shower. Do we have an umbrella? Of course not. Eventually the rain stops, the sun reappears and the air is filled with steamy cow-dung-scented condensation as the dog dries out. We reach the far side of the field of cows, where a notice on the gate informs us "The cattle grazing in this field are Aberdeen Angus Highland bulls. They are completely docile and harmless." By this time, Mother is more at risk of being trampled by her shattered, wet, starving daughter.

The path now leads through another small copse, emerging into very pretty scenery. Heavily scented shrubs and a variety of colourful flowers fill the borders of a large area of plush, newly-mowed grass. It's almost like someone's garden. Only when we come to a fluffy rabbit in a hutch and observe an enraged figure flapping his arms like a bird of prey ready for the kill do we realise it *is* someone's garden.

'Do you realise you're on private property?' It becomes apparent we have inadvertently wandered into the local vicarage plot and the vicar is not pleased. He strides towards us angrily, robes flying; face rapidly turning crimson above his dog collar. I feel a bubble of laughter rising but manage to suppress it.

'I'm sorry,' I attempt. 'We're not familiar with the area and didn't realise we'd taken the wrong path.'

But the vicar is on a roll. 'How would you like it if I decided to have a Sunday picnic in your garden?'

The mental image of this large country vicar eating cucumber sandwiches on our postage-stamp-sized council house lawn, with the ethnic and mad Irish neighbours peering over the fence is too much for me and the bubble of hysteria bursts.

'Damned tourists,' the vicar concludes as he shoos us off his property.

'I thought you were supposed to help lost souls,' I retort, making a mental note never to donate to Christian Aid again.

Back on track, my spirits lift as the town of Ventnor comes into view. Crossing an extensive car park to find a much needed public convenience, Boo decides to develop the psychological bad leg that always accompanies the sight of gravel. Hauling a muddy bundle of wriggling canine, stinking of wet dog and cow manure into the toilets, is of course, my sole responsibility, as is the delightful task of cleaning her up sufficiently to be allowed inside a pub. Are there any paper towels in the loos? Of course not. The only available wiping material we have is the swimsuit I intended to wear on the beach. I cringe as I carry out my cleaning duties, making another mental note to ensure Mother buys me the most expensive replacement I can find when, or if, we get home.

We step through the doors of The Blenheim Hotel looking like twin scarecrows from The Wizard of Oz, our stinky Toto now securely leashed.

'I'll have to sit down.' Mother sinks into the nearest seat. 'You get us something to eat and drink. I'm exhausted.' Yes Mother, no Mother, three bags full Mother.

'Two halves of Guinness and two cheese salad rolls please.' I manage a smile for the Landlord.

'I'm sorry my dear, we stopped serving five minutes ago.'

Perfect timing is another of my family's traits, but that's another story I'm too knackered to tell right now.

A DOG IS FOR CHRISTMAS

Castle Rock

Stark contrasts dominate Nottingham's famous castle grounds. Urban and rural, ancient and modern, affluent and underprivileged, dawdle and hustle are all apparent from this spot. The intrusive noise of a city intermingling with the gentle humming of nature. Industrial, dusty fumes invading the ozone-filled air of the castle grounds.

In the far distance an uneven horizon; a patchwork of various shades of green, interspersed with the occasional garish splash of yellow; the odour of rape not discernible from this distance, but stored in the memory and equally as repulsive as its colour. Pylons, spires, cranes and industrial chimneys reach up into the vast stretch of sky, mottled with lazily drifting clouds. The labours of the city discernible from this distance; workmen drilling, lorries unloading, the grinding of machinery as another bin is emptied into the jaws of the evil-stinking refuse collection vehicle.

Historical churches mingle with modern monstrosities, high rise car parks and offices merge with solid brick and stone buildings. A contemporary housing estate nestles by the side of old terraced houses, Victorian bay windows glistening in the sun. Gaudy coloured cars and buses speed along roads or stand motionless in traffic jams, impatiently honking horns. The roar of a motor bike as it zigzags through the queue, elsewhere the sound of skidding. Sirens peaking and fading almost constantly become just an accepted part of the hectic pace of a twenty-first century city. A high speed train rushes into the station, while in the distance the sails of Green's Windmill rotate at a leisurely pace in the breeze. The "Trip to Jerusalem'"offers a range of beers or spirits to its many visitors; opposite a Chinese restaurant displays a menu of tempting oriental dishes. The past and the present fused together in a city buzzing with life. The fusty tang of age and timelessness outweighing that of synthetic, modern life.

At four, a nearby church chimes a jaunty tune, followed shortly by the resounding boom of the Council House clock. Which is correct and who really knows, or cares for that matter? Lives are beginning and ending in the clinical smelling wards of the University hospital to the left, while details of those somewhere in between are stored in the musty records filed in the offices of County Hall, to the right.

Close by, the elegant castle, steeped in history, stands overlooking the city. Tourists stroke the uneven, stone surface of the walls; tiny fingers outline the names carved in statues as childish voices struggle to read aloud the unfamiliar names. The castle is surrounded by shrubs of varying shades, grassy banks, colourful flower beds and majestic trees. The subtle scents of laburnum, bluebells, horse chestnut blossom and liverwort assaulting the nostrils like a sweet, yet bitter-tinged spring bouquet. Passers-by tentatively caress the sticky leaves of unusual plants in the borders, sucking in breath when camouflaged nettles sting.

The wind whispers secrets old and new in the branches, newly adorned with fresh spring leaves. A child traces her small hand over the gnarled trunk of an oak tree, stroking the smooth bumps then withdrawing from the sharp points of surrounding bark. Birds of many varieties go about their business in the peaceful surroundings. A pigeon basks in the sunshine, cooing softly. A female blackbird wrestles with a defiant worm, a tasty supper for her, while the handsome partner looks on trilling his enthusiastic song. Squawking rooks take flight from an ancient cypress tree; their flapping wings alarming a nearby toddler, sending her scurrying back to her family. A fresh rush of tears and wailing as her mouth-watering ice-cream plops onto the path, but soon pacified enfolded in her mother's soft arms as she offers reassuring words and the promise of a replacement.

People of all ages and nationalities wander from the gatehouse to the castle entrance, or sit pensively on wooden benches, enjoying a sandwich or snack. Everywhere the buzz of human voices, conferring, laughing, squabbling, enquiring, in a rich variety of languages and accents. The pungent whiff of foreign cigarette smoke drifts in the breeze. Love struck young couples, families, pensioners, Goths and the lonely all find solace here. Groups of foreigners pose by statues, hands caressing the smooth stone, lips smiling, as someone records the moment for posterity with the tiny click of a camera button.

A child's kite tugs on the end of a length of string over the castle green, tail beating rhythmically as a captivated youngster giggles infectiously. Young feet scuttle excitedly along the paths, others shuffle softly, stiletto heels click unsteadily over the uneven stone slabs towards the castle doors. People recline on cold metal chairs outside the café sipping tea or quenching thirsts with fresh fruit juice. The aroma of freshly brewed coffee wafts from the open doors, amalgamating with the subtle scent of sun on warm skin. An elderly lady sits alone, a spoon tinkling against the side of her cup as she stirs absently, her thoughts obviously elsewhere. She wraps her woollen scarf around her more tightly as the sun disappears temporarily behind a mass of darkening cloud.

The last of spring blossom dances on the slab stones, fresh green ferns wait to unfurl and the spongy moss of decades clings to the castle walls. By the empty bandstand a young couple sit on a weathered bench, fingers entwined, oblivious to the roughness of the splintered wood as they talk softly; eyes locked in the newness of love. Her exotic heady perfume a contrast to the spicy fragrance of his cologne, yet neither as sweet as the lingering scent of new mown grass. Dappled shadows of trees quiver on the pathways like monochrome kaleidoscope patterns. A feather spirals lazily from the branch of a chestnut tree; a sycamore leaf drifts across the grass, buffeted by the gentle wind. The snap of a twig as a stranger passes, the gentle kiss of a courting couple, the soft buzz of insects and the creak of the gate as another visitor escapes from the city turmoil to the sanctuary of the castle grounds. Peace prevails.

A Dog Is For Christmas

There is no post this morning but canines are pre-programmed to bark viciously at the letter box at unearthly hours in the morning so the family, as always , are rudely blasted from sleep before they are ready. I crawl reluctantly from my warm bed, nursing a hangover and attempt to force a smile.

Ablutions completed and seasonal salutations all round (humbug) my first task this Christmas morning is to feed the birds. I empty the bag of goodies onto the bird table and turn to walk back to the house. I notice several piles of doggy dirt on the lawn. What better way to start Christmas day than with a bit of shovelling I muse. That way, surely, things can only get better.

Hands thoroughly washed, I begin the preparations for dinner. This year I have excelled myself by preparing home made pate for starters as opposed to opening a can of soup. The pate is arranged artistically on seven plates around the table, complete with neat little side salads. Everything is under control so we decide to open our presents.

Our first Christmas with pooch taught us not to put his presents under the tree along with the rest. That particular Christmas morning we arose to find the floor covered in scraps of wrapping paper and a very overstuffed hound. These days we are wiser and keep his stocking hidden from sight until the last moment. Tail wagging furiously, tongue lolling, eyes gleaming; he sets about opening his gifts. This takes approximately thirty seconds after which he gives us that "Is that all?" look and saunters away leaving paper, squeaky toys and chews scattered all over the lounge floor. The rest of the family open their gifts with more decorum and appreciation.

I return to the kitchen to continue preparations to find seven plates of neat little side salad minus pate and a very replete looking dog licking his chops. "God bless Mr Heinz," I mutter, quickly emptying cans of soup into a saucepan.

Dinner is scheduled for precisely one o clock, as always, as my dear brother-in-law has an appointment with the golf course as soon as he can escape. He arrives on the dot, leaving his eighty-eight year old mother to find her own way up the slippery path unaided. The pooch goes into a frenzy; he cannot for some reason abide the man and makes this quite apparent. Actually, I quite empathise with the dog but am in no position to disappear under the table and snarl. My fixed grin is precariously slipping as I serve the dinner. My brother-in-law says he doesn't want stuffing. The dog and I would disagree. He leaves to play his solitary round whilst swallowing the last spoonful of his pudding. We probably won't see him for another year; thank God for small mercies.

After dinner I escape with the dog for a planned long walk in the countryside in order to miss Her Majesty pontificating from the Palace. Peace and solitude at last; I have looked forward to it for days. We set off; the dog walks a hundred yards, poops (I scoop) then turns about. Paws firmly fixed he refuses to budge another inch. I return to the house just in time for the royal speech; maybe pooch has heard a rumour that the corgis are to put in a guest appearance.

The Queen informs us that it is Christmas and that Jesus was born at this time. I am intrigued by the fact that her speech on the radio in the kitchen is ahead of the one on the television. How does she do that? The prospect of washing all those pots in the sink suddenly seems quite appealing. I return to the kitchen to find the dog has thrown up on the doorstep and then attempted to bury it with the doormat, bless him. I spend a happy half an hour cleaning up vomit and hundreds of doormat tufts. I don't think I fancy those chicken sandwiches now.

Evening falls and it's time to settle down in front of the television with a drink or seven. Just as I become interested in a gripping drama, the dog decides to investigate his presents again. He decides he rather likes the plucked latex chicken with the extraordinarily loud squeak. After two hours of throwing it for him to retrieve, the television inaudible now, I have a strong urge to use up the leftover stuffing but am unsure whether to use it on the latex chicken or the dog. I think I'll have another drink and no doubt another hangover tomorrow. Still, we all know the cure for that; the hair of the dog, what else?

Bonchurch

Step from the ferry on to the Isle of Wight and you are immediately taken back in time. Take a walk through Luccombe Chine from Shanklin and you'll feel you're in a different era completely. In summer it's impossible to feel harassed or rushed as you stroll through woodland leading to footpaths where hydrangeas grow in profusion and the air is filled with the sweet scents of old-fashioned cottage gardens. Pause a while for tea and cream scones at a café tucked away almost like a secret garden, then if you have the courage, climb to the top of the rock and set your imagination free as you sit in the wishing chair. The pathways lead eventually to the sleepy town of Ventnor, but between the two lies the tiny village of Bonchurch, a place so exquisitely unspoiled and pretty it could be the setting from a fairy tale.

There are only three essentials for your visit to this magical little place; time, a camera and a good pair of lungs. You may also like to bring along a bag of crusts, some loose change and a copy of your favourite poem. A small place it may be, but nowhere can you escape the charm, tranquillity and history that are the essence of Bonchurch.

Begin your tour from the sheltered shingle and sand beach, making sure you spend a little time exploring the pools surrounding the craggy rocks. Lack of pollution ensures there's an abundance of marine life to scrutinise and many varied shells for the collector to gather. Then commence the steep climb past a row of quaint, thatched cottages with well-tended, colourful gardens. Worth getting out that camera while you catch your breath. Shortly, you'll step into a small copse where a welcome wooden bench beckons you to stay awhile. Bonchurch is mentioned in the Doomsday book and is believed to have been one of the earliest settlements on the island due to the natural spring water which gurgles freely just in front of where you are seated. Keep that camera handy for if you are very still you may capture a variety of birds and butterflies on film and may even be fortunate enough to witness a red squirrel.

Continue your journey through the copse; gaze up to the dizzying heights of the treetops, refusing to reveal even a wisp of blue sky and feel the charge of Mother Nature flowing up through the soles of your feet from the rich, springy earth.

Another steep climb will lead you to the old church, built during the reign of William the Conqueror. A creaky metal gate takes you into the churchyard, a mass of lichen-covered, uneven gravestones, yet so peaceful it's tempting to sit and meditate for hours. Many of the inscriptions on the older tombstones are virtually indecipherable but you will find six Swinburne graves, including that of Algernon, the poet. The spirit of the past cannot be ignored and with the open sea before you, it's as if some strange force draws you into the church. It's a gentle pull, but very persuasive. The heavy, ancient wooden door leads into a very small, musty scented church, almost like something from the world of Lilliput. Sit for a while to pray or if you prefer, just contemplate, then before you leave write your name, worries and concerns in the visitor's book. You never know, the atmosphere here is enough to convince even the most devout atheist there may be some truth in the power of prayer.

Leaving the church you will see two magnificent mansions. To your left is "Winterbourne," now a hotel and restaurant but once occupied by Charles Dickens. It is told he wrote six chapters of David Copperfield here and may have taken Bonchurch people as role models for his characters. To the right is "East Dene," an elegant stone building dating back to the middle ages, once the home of the poet Algernon

Swinburne and now owned by an educational trust offering leisure courses.

Continue upwards, the climb becoming increasingly steeper, but a rest at the Bonchurch Inn is a worthwhile reward. The sort of pub more mature visitors will remember from the past, complete with old piano, table games and black and white photographs of famous visitors. The beer and food are first-rate and you may be fortunate to drop in when one of the poetry reading sessions is taking place. If you're confident enough, join in and read aloud your favourite piece; you might make a lasting impression on the locals.

Onward and upward to the next bend, where a climb up the steps through the rock known as Devil's Chimney brings you out onto the main road of Upper Bonchurch. The going seems hard, but there's compensation at the top and a downhill walk to follow. Hopefully, your camera is a digital one capable of holding many frames, as the views from here across Boniface Down and Ventnor will demand you capture their magnificence from every angle.

The return journey down to the village is plain sailing by comparison, descending the steep and narrow Chimney steps, then after a short flat walk, take the 101 flight of steps leading to the village pond. Surrounded by huge and varied trees, a perfect spot to recharge and relax while feeding the many varieties of ducks and the huge carp which rise from the depths when visitors throw sustenance. If you didn't bring any then for a small price, the combined village shop and Post Office opposite will supply a ready prepared pack of fodder for their pond residents. The upkeep of and supplies for the pond are all supplied by local inhabitants. Sit for a while on the stone wall surrounding the pond and you'll almost hear the gossip shared by those who sat in the same spot many generations ago.

A walk to the East along the Village Road will also require you to pause and take more photographs. The pond, the only village shop, the grotto, the drinking fountain and the quaint yellow-tinted stone cottages covered in creepers and sweet honeysuckle are all images you'll want to record for posterity. Once at the end of the road, a sharp decline will lead you back to the starting point on the shore.

The shadow of the past will have made a big impression on you; it is inescapable in every part of Bonchurch. You can feel it as you walk around the village, see it in the buildings and hear it in the legends and stories. As Charles Dickens wrote, "Bonchurch is the prettiest place I ever saw in my life, at home or abroad." Despite the effort involved you'll be both relaxed and invigorated. And if you're still not tired you may want turn around and to do the whole thing again in reverse.

GONE WITH THE WINE

Table Relationships

Dear Grandma,

I've been thinking about you today; it being your one hundred and fourteenth birthday and a Sunday too. Being a God-fearing woman you always loved Sundays didn't you? I hope He's all you envisioned Him to be now you're actually residing in His hometown. Can you recall those Sunday dinners we used to have at your house? I remember so well the smell of the joint sizzling in its pan surrounded by roast potatoes you never see the likes of today in these times of fat-free meat. I can taste them as I write. I'm sorry I was such a pain about the sprouts and the mashed potato. I couldn't help being a fussy eater; unlike my dustbin of a big sister who would, and still will, eat anything and everything put in front of her.

You see Grandma; I always felt she was the favoured one just because of her voracious appetite. I was so envious she got to sit next to Granddad at the table while I was always pinned between you and Mum so you could watch and nag me from both sides as we fought the battle of the Brussels. You even put newspaper down in front of them to protect your tablecloth and it became a family joke. Every meal my sister would smile up at granddad as she uttered those immortal words.

'We're dirty boys aren't we Granddad?'

I never got any newspaper; just admonished for every crumb and gravy stain I left on your precious tablecloth. Forgive me for saying this, but I sometimes wonder if you thought more of that tablecloth than you did of your family. I could never understand why you got so annoyed; it was always washed religiously (excuse the pun) the following day regardless of whether it was dirty or clean. "Cleanliness is next to Godliness" was always your motto.

'Don't stand still in our house on a Monday,' our granddad used to joke. 'You'll get washed in the Dolly tub along with everything else.'

I remember walking home from school on Mondays with a feeling of dread I'm sure no child of such a tender age should experience. Opening the back door into the scullery and being overpowered by the damp, steamy smell of washing day was a weekly experience I despised. By that time you would be on your last load, bent over the tub with your ponch and washboard, tired and irritable after a day spent scrubbing everything in the house that could be washed. Hot water boiling in the copper, sheets pegged out and drying on the line in the back yard and piles of starched laundry on almost every available surface. I hated it and I hated the inevitable meal that would follow. The tablecloth, always first in the tub, was returned to the table pristine, unstained and still warm from the iron when I came in from school.

The only good thing about Mondays was the mouse. I always wanted a dog, you knew that, but it wasn't allowed, so a small white mouse was purchased in an attempt to pacify me. The mouse and cage had to be kept in the scullery of course, but on Mondays you always moved it into the dining room while you performed your weekly washing rituals. As you mangled, pegged out your last load and then got down on your hands and knees to scrub the red-tiled scullery floor you didn't know that I would furtively remove the mouse from its cage and play with it on your freshly laundered tablecloth. I loved stroking its shiny soft fur and watching it scamper illicitly, almost camouflaged over the table. I'd been doing it for months without you ever finding out until that particular Monday. Do you remember it still?

Washing completed, floor scrubbed and mouse safely returned to its cage, we sat around the table for the Monday meal. The leftover meat, now cold and leathery, the enemy sprouts and mash now disguised as bubble and squeak alongside the dreaded cold pickles. Red Cabbage, gherkins, pickled onions and the ultimate of horrors, contributed by our American father, the stuffed olives. We only had them because my sister loved them. Another family story told around the table every Monday was that my sister's first word had been "Ollum" and not Mummy or Daddy. I wonder what mine was? Probably "NO" if the truth be told. I remember trying to get in everyone's good books by attempting to consume just one olive every Monday evening. But to this day I still hate their bitter, salty taste and have never managed to swallow one yet. Whenever my now beloved sister comes to stay I always buy a jar of olives for her. After large quantities of alcohol I sometimes bravely attempt to eat one but the result is still the same as it was back then. Spitting out half chewed olives didn't help my popularity at the meal table.

Anyway, I can still see the family sitting round the table that Monday evening. Granddad and sister on the opposite side, tucking into their meal with relish, laughing and joking about their newspaper placemats. Our dad to their left, quiet and unassuming, probably not daring to speak for fear of getting his head bitten off by mum. Nothing ever changed on that front either, grandma. I was, as usual, attempting to force down an acceptable amount of the meal so as to be excused from the table when I spotted it. Right in the middle of the table between you and my sister a pile of dark mouse droppings contrasting sharply against the snowy white tablecloth. I knew it would only be a matter of time before your hawk eyes spotted it too.

'What on earth is that? ' You suddenly snapped, pointing at the offending blobs. My sister stuck out her chubby arm and picked some up. I don't blame you for being angry with me. But your wrath paled into insignificance compared to the feeling of pleasure I derived watching my sister's face.

Believing that anything she discovered on the table must be edible, she greedily devoured the droppings. We still laugh about it now.

Your still loving, but not quite so fussy granddaughter.

Gone With The Wine

Dear Scarlett,

I started reading "Gone with the Wind" today. I love your strong impulsive character; a girl after my own heart if ever there was one. Mind you, I must say I can't see the attraction in that Ashley Wilkes; far too timid and indecisive for you. I'm not particularly worried as it's obvious you're idolised by every male in the district and I'm convinced someone will come along to turn your head away from the insipid Ashley. I'll enjoy my coffee and fig roll imagining the wonderful romantic affair the future surely holds for you. My washing basket's full, but I'll think about that tomorrow.

Tuesday's arrived and I've been reading more of your story. I can understand you being angry with Rhett Butler initially, but can't you see he's the perfect match for you? The Civil War's created awful conditions; I can empathise with your revulsion at nursing those dying soldiers. But Rhett did offer to take you away from it all. How could you turn him down? He secures a horse and carriage for you, risks life and limb helping you escape the dangers of Gettysburg, confesses he loves you and what do you do? Tell him you hate and despise him! I know he's no saint Scarlett, but you're no angel either if you don't mind me saying so. I just hope you see sense soon. I'll have a drop of whisky in my coffee today; I feel a bit edgy. The washing basket's overflowing now and the sink's full of dirty pots, but I'll think about that tomorrow.

Wednesday's come round fast. I didn't sleep well last night and feel tired today. A bit tearful too. Your journey back to Tara with sickly Melanie upset me but I suppose under the circumstances I'll forgive you for whipping that poor horse until it dropped. I've poured a glass of wine to calm my nerves but it's rapidly disappearing as I read that your mother is dead, your father has lost his marbles and Tara is in a state of disrepair. I know you have the determination to restore her to her former glory, but things don't look good right now, especially with that Yankee soldier lying dead at the bottom of your stairs. you sure made a mess of his face when you shot him Scarlett. My wine glass is empty, my sink and washing basket are still brimming and surfaces need dusting, but I'll think about that tomorrow.

I've a thick head this morning; it's a very dull looking Thursday so I'll just read today. I can't believe your father has gone; what a terrible riding accident and how tragic for you. But marrying Sue Ellen's beau Frank, in order to pay your taxes is a bit heartless. Now look what's happened. You're attacked by thieves in your carriage, Frank's killed trying to seek revenge and you end up a widow again. Just how many men are going to expire before you realise you should be with the enigmatic Mr Butler? My wine bottle's drained; my washing basket and sink are still full, the layer of dust is thickening and the grass needs mowing, but I'll think about that tomorrow.

It's Friday already. Congratulations, Scarlett. At long last you've agreed to marry Rhett, though I suspect it's more for money than love. How kind and considerate he is; comforting you when you have nightmares, returning to Tara when you become home sick and even presenting Mammy with that beautiful red petticoat. What a charmer. And now you have a beautiful daughter too. Look what a fine family you have and how happy you've made Rhett. I think I'll crack open some champagne and celebrate before reading on. Cheers.

What on earth are you doing? Put that photo of Ashley down. Why are you thinking of him when everything is perfect? I can't believe you've decided against more children just because you want your figure back. Depriving a man like Rhett of his oats can only lead to disaster. I can't stand any more today. Maybe we'll both think more clearly after a good night's sleep. I've opened the champagne so I suppose I'll have to finish it off or it'll go flat. I hope it drowns my sorrows. It won't get the washing, dusting, hoovering or gardening done, but I'll think about that tomorrow.

Thank goodness it's the weekend now. I had to go shopping this morning as there was no food left in the cupboards, but I felt so depressed I bought a bottle of brandy instead. It was the shock of reading about your fall and losing the baby you were carrying as a result of your one night of passion with Rhett after that party. I honestly believed things might turn out right after that. I didn't think they could get much worse. But now I'm sobbing because Bonnie has been taken from you and Rhett is out of his mind with grief. I can't see the print too well what with the tears and the brandy but I just have to finish this book.

Poor frail Melanie has lost her fight now but wonder of wonders, you have finally realised it's not Ashley who floats your boat, but Rhett. I'm convinced he'll take you back with open arms and all will be well. But now it seems the promise of a happy ending is as empty as my brandy bottle. There's no food in the house and they've just been to cut my gas off as I forgot to pay the bill. Maybe it's a blessing in disguise as I was contemplating putting my head in the oven. I can't face the washing basket, pots, dusting or hoovering. The grass is six inches long and the borders full of weeds. The bin needs emptying and all these bottles need recycling. But frankly my dear, I don't give a damn.

In Deepest Sympathy,
Your Inebriated Friend.

P.S. Good luck with Tara. I'd offer to help you but my own house needs putting in order when I've sobered up.

Just Browsing

Dear Fosseway Writers Group,

I recently stumbled across your latest writing competition and noticed that entries had to be written in epistolary format. It caught my attention as I've always enjoyed writing letters. Since my wife Edie passed away I've not had much interest in anything, but a tiny flicker of enthusiasm crept into the mantle of grief that has embodied me since she departed. I read all the information and rules, but then it dawned on me that in these times it's more common to communicate digitally. Don't get me wrong, I've nothing against technology, though I don't use it much myself as I'm getting on in years and am probably considered a technological dinosaur in this ever evolving world. I still remember the times when letters were hand written on stationary with a fountain pen, then sealed in an envelope. I can recall the experience of licking the stamp then walking to post the letter in a mail box, so you can deduce from that I'm far removed from today's methods of communication.

It saddens me people are no longer taught the art of writing a proper letter as Edie and I were back in our school days. I sometimes wonder what is taught in schools nowadays. It seems to me without their phones and tablets, the majority of youngsters would be unable to tell the time or cope with any mathematical problem or monetary matter. I believe they'd also lose their way every time they went out as they have no idea about directions or maps now they all have one of those satnav things or ask Siri, whoever he is. And don't get me started on proper English. I mean, grammar, spelling, punctuation all seem to have gone out the window nowadays. All these messages and texts in a language my generation can barely understand, and all this gobbledegook they speak since technology took over. In our day the Amazon was a river, web designers were spiders and trolls lived under bridges. Birds were the only things that could tweet, spam was something we were forced to eat and a swipe was something you got if you misbehaved in school, probably followed by another once you arrived home. So I'm thinking most of the entries for this competition will be presented in modern compositions sent via emails, texts, I.M's, blogs, tweets and other such technological tools. It wouldn't surprise me if some of them are even written by robots. I did Google all about A.I once but concluded I don't want a co pilot or a digitalised assistant in my life. I'd love to have my Edie back though, but technology can't do anything about that yet as far as I'm aware.

Anyway, back to letters. As I said, I've always enjoyed writing them as well as receiving. As a child it was the highlight of every morning waiting to see what would drop through the letter box, be it a letter from a relative, a penpal overseas, a postcard from someone on holiday or an invitation to a party.

I wonder if children today receive anything by snail mail, as they call it. As far as I can see they spend almost all their free time staring at phones, tablets and screens. My own family are much the same. They live down south, but we used to see them quite a bit when the grandkids were little and Edie was here to cook meals and entertain them. But after we lost her, my daughter said I needed a computer to help me cope alone, so now we use FaceTime. It's okay, but I'm not sure I'd recognise my grandkids any longer. I've forgotten what colour their eyes are since they had those V.R. headsets and can only identify them by the designs on their phone cases these days. I think they'd only recognise me if I had a rectangular frame round my head. Still, it's better than nothing and as my daughter says it saves on fuel and it's kinder to the environment than driving here.

Even when they go out they're attached to their devices. You see them in those fast food restaurants sitting round the table glued to their phones. No conversation at all. And I wonder if anyone can actually cook these days as they all seem to eat out or send out for takeaways. Edie and I loved to visit fancy restaurants on special occasions, but most of the time you couldn't beat her good old home cooking. After Edie died my daughter said I'd never manage to cook like her Mum, but even I can manage to pop those ready meals I get delivered with my online shopping in the microwave she insisted on getting me. I had to look up the instructions on Youtube though, like I do with a lot of things, but I'm learning. I must remember to ask that Alexa thing in the kitchen to find me some easy recipes I can manage, just to prove my daughter wrong.

They even meet their partners on the Internet these days. I said to Maisie on the Bereavement Forum this afternoon that we didn't need any dating sites or Timber, or whatever it's called in our day. I met my Edie one Saturday night at the local dancehall and Maisie said she'd met Jim in the shop where she worked. She's nice is Maisie. I've never met her, but we chat about all sorts of things. She sent me a photo and I sent her one of me and we laughed and said we ought to meet really because we've heard all about people pretending to be somebody else on the Internet and we should check each other out. I doubt we will though. Like me, Maisie was devoted to her partner and we're not looking for replacements. No one could match my Edie and anyway, I don't want to risk being catfished.

And we managed to have kids without sexting, sending emoticons of aubergines, or swapping photos of our body parts. Makes me wonder if they'll reproduce online before long to avoid the inconvenience of leaving the house to meet, the risks associated with intercourse, and the pain of childbirth.

Edie and I used to love going to the theatre, the cinema and dancing to live bands. At home we had one television with three channels, a radio and a record player. Everything's gone virtual these days. All this streaming; music, films, sport, news, games and even books. Edie and I loved to read and visited the library every week. Our local one is under threat of closing now which would be a real shame. I made sure I signed the petition on their website to save it. I listened to a podcast the other day about how much things have changed since my day and how writers from the past had predicted all these things. I read 'Brave New World' and '1984' at school, but I'd never heard of the one called 'Neuromancer' that actually predicted cyberspace and hacking. I've downloaded it onto my Kindle now.

Edie and I always used to write letters to each other when we were apart. They kept us going through some tough times and I've never parted with them. I think they're in a box under the bed somewhere, but I'm not sure I could read them now she's gone. We were sticklers for writing letters of complaint as well. Some strong words might have been exchanged, but It was only between you and the person you were complaining about or the company. Nowadays, they all put their grievances and opinions on social media sites and it gets out of hand, people swearing and threatening each other, then going off at tangents arguing about anything. I posted about it the other day. I said everybody's entitled to their opinion, but I don't think it necessary to use foul language, air all your dirty laundry, rant about neighbours, display your road rage or kick off about things you don't understand and that I thought it was about time they showed some respect and restraint instead of putting these things all over the web. I got more than 500 comments on that one, most of them rude and offensive, telling me I should keep my opinions to myself and bog off back to the museum or my care home. I have no plans to stop though. I know my rights and can point them to the right website to confirm it.

Anyway, I'm having second thoughts about entering your competition because an ordinary letter isn't going to impress anyone. I might come along to the meeting where you read out all the winners though. I'd like to hear what's popular these days. Come to think of it though, I haven't been out much lately for some reason and I am a bit wary. I mean, there's some strange folk out there and you can never be sure if people are talking to themselves or whether they've got those things in their ears they attach to phones. I daren't drive after I read on Facebook that all the roads are full of pot holes and if I walked I've read the paving slabs are all loose and uneven and I don't need a nasty fall at my age. It's not like you can get to see a doctor any more. You have to do it all online and then you get a telephone appointment to discuss your problem. I had one a bit back and the doc asked if I could upload a photo of my condition. I asked him if he'd ever lived alone and tried to snap a shot of his haemorrhoids.

Then there's all this antisocial behaviour, knife crime, drugs and abuse you read about online. I'm not sure I'd feel safe one way and another. I'm hoping I'll be able to read the winning entries on your website though, so maybe it's best to do that.

I'll finish here as I haven't done my daily Wordle or Suduko and I"m expecting a parcel from Evri anytime soon. I had to order a new keyboard as a lot of the keys on mine are indecipherable for some reason. I always used to look forward to a chat with the delivery driver as I don't have many visitors since Edie passed, but these days he doesn't seem to have much time. Just drops the parcel, takes a photo and rushes off. Then they expect you to rate the delivery as well as the company and the item you've purchased. I wouldn't be surprised if it reaches the point where you get a 'How did we do?' email after you've been to a public convenience. 'How many stars would you give the design of the toilet, the thickness of the toilet paper and the flush?' Honestly. I swear technology is taking over the world, but I'm not going to get sucked in I tell you.

Maybe I'll download that pro writing aid app you recommended later just in case I do enter your competition. There's so many apps to plough through now that sometimes it takes me ages to find the right one. I even came across one the other day that tells you how much time you spend on the internet, but it's not accurate. There's no way I waste six and a half hours out of my busy life every day on technology. I've far better things to do.

Yours Sincerely, Harold Luddite

PITCH PERFECT

Split Ends

I don't know what's happened to Rita. She's completely changed. Whereas once she was an extrovert; unpredictable and stunning, she's now become quite homely and unattractive. She's lost her sparkle; turned into someone ordinary and dull. Once a fascinating conversationalist, she now has little to say and rarely puts in an appearance. Okay, she may have done a few outrageous things in the past, not all of them legal, but at least she was someone you couldn't ignore. Now, no one would give her a second glance or even notice she existed. I don't know why she's changed so much; maybe it's the medication she takes or the therapy she's receiving. I'm not sure I like these changes; maybe it's time we got rid of her. No one could possibly be interested in her lack lustre personality and the inactive life she now leads. I can't live with someone plain and uninteresting so I suppose she'll have to go.

The problem is Rita has been with us for as far back as I can remember and it's difficult to let go. She doesn't fit in with us any longer but to exclude her is scary; as if part of me has died. I'm frightened that the others will turn the same way; bland, stay at home types with no drive or purpose. It's unthinkable that we might all fade away into nothingness and then what would be left? Will we all disappear completely or even worse just be left as one boring homely person like Rita? I don't think I could live with that.

I imagine the doctor will be pleased I'm giving up one of my alter egos; maybe it is the beginning of my recovery from this strange condition. If it is I'm not so sure I like it.

Departures

Abandoned coffee mugs, skim forming on the surface. Boxer shorts strewn haphazardly on the bedroom floor, always inside out. Greasy frying pans dumped in the kitchen sink after a morning fry up. The sound of ecstatic football fans and hysterical commentators from a too loud television. The faint aroma of beer and kebabs lingering from a lad's night on the tiles. Heavy metal, rap, hip hop and punk blaring from oversized speakers. It's strange the things you miss when they fly the nest.

Spreading their wings they took flight leaving me alone with only snoring at night and nose blowing in the morning for company. Black socks and white trainers, untidy stubble and a comb over, out of tune whistling accompanying annoying country songs, a constant presence hogging the remote, crisp crunching during intense dramas, too much complaining and brooding, too little laughter and song. A cosy little love nest the first time we were just a couple, replaced by irritation when left together with no hatchlings.

But then he too left. Falling from his perch quite suddenly and unexpectedly, leaving behind unfinished business and out of date documents, odd socks just in case, rusty tools and stiff paintbrushes, golf clubs, squash rackets, cricket bats neglected by arthritis and time, echoing rooms and howling silence, unforeseen heartache and loneliness, too much choice and too little purpose.

No longer a spring chicken, now I must flit. A cage in the aviary for old birds with broken wings and ruffled feathers waits for me. The only eggs hard boiled in blackened saucepans, the only songs from bygone eras warbled by jaded occupants of soggy armchairs in the community room. I leave behind an empty nest for sale or rent, carpets, curtains and misty memories included.

Pitch Perfect

My piano teacher tells me to watch as she plays a simple tune. Her slender, elegant fingers dance across the keys creating perfection. The hands of a pianist. I stare at my own fingers; short and stubby, better suited to catching, saving goals.

Now it's my turn. I've not practiced much. I take a deep breath and stare at the music sheet in front of me. The black notes seem to glare back at me as if they know I don't understand them. I stumble through the short piece, probably hitting half the notes incorrectly. It ends. My teacher gives me a withering look.

Mummy arrives to collect me. Mummy wants me to be a piano player, but I'd rather play football with Daddy. Mummy pays the teacher and we say goodbye. Mummy says she'll bring me again next week. Same day, same time.

I tell Mummy my teacher doesn't think I'm very good at playing the piano. Mummy says I will get better with practice. I take a deep breath and tell Mummy as gently as I can that I don't want to play the piano and would rather play football with Daddy.

Mummy stops in her tracks and looks me straight in the eye. She tells me she doesn't know when I'll see Daddy again. When I ask why she frowns and says he's playing away. A tear sneaks onto her cheek as she turns her face. She must be missing Daddy just like I am.

I can't wait to see Daddy even if it's not for a while. I'll have to be patient. It must be an important match if he's gone a long way away to play in it. I hope his team win and he'll teach me to be as good as he is. Maybe then Mummy will cancel my piano lessons and smile again.

Close Shave

He'd given up on finding love. At his age he'd resigned himself to living out his last years alone. He'd only looked at the website out of curiosity and boredom. Nothing on the box and the lodgers all out courting, he'd resorted to the computer and been drawn in by the photograph of a real beauty. Stunning green eyes, petite but perfectly proportioned, serious expression yet hinting at mischief, he was immediately smitten. He'd read her profile and already felt they belonged together.

He'd become a bit of a recluse over the years and was wary of mixing with others as he felt they'd judge him; conclude he was weird or just plain crazy. He had expected to remain a hermit with just his uninvited guests as company. But now, he realised they were the ones holding him back and much as he hadn't strongly objected to them moving in originally, he now realised if he wanted to start afresh they'd have to go. He wasn't a cruel man and would openly admit he'd grown fond of them all, but now he must think of himself for a change. Besides, they'd soon all be expecting again and he was getting too old to deal with babysitting and all the hassle of raising youngsters.

First he confirmed a date to visit his potential new companion, then carefully composed his own advertisement.
'Free to a good home. Two owls, one hen, four larks and a wren. All preparing to roost. Nests supplied.'

Then he headed for the bathroom and spent a long time shaving off the beard he'd carried around with its bizarre contents for years. After all, he didn't want his new kitten to get its little claws caught up in it.

Prima Donna

Her name is Donna and she's perfect. Look at her; flawless facial features, long, shiny golden hair tumbling down her back, beautiful hour-glass figure and slender, shapely legs right up to her bottom, as my grandma used to say. I miss my grandma and her funny expressions. My grandma would have hated Donna as much as I do. But you're not allowed to voice any contempt for Donna; she's everyone's darling, you know.

Darling Donna; so immaculately turned out. So clean and sweet-smelling, her hair tied back in a thick pony-tail that dances as she walks. She even makes walking look like something only she can do correctly. Perfectly measured steps, spine as rigid and upright as a fireman's pole, she'd make a catwalk model look ungainly.

And that smile. It never seems to leave her face; fixed there, dazzling everything and everyone in her path. I wonder if she smiles in her sleep. Are her dreams full of enchantment and magical journeys or does she ever wake up screaming from terrifying nightmares as I do? She deserves to, but I suspect her conscience is as clear and unblemished as her complexion.

What makes her perfection even more convincing is the way she pretends she's unaware of her own qualities and how caring and giving she is to everyone, regardless of their station in life. Attentive, reassuring, enthusiastic even in the most disturbing circumstances; doesn't anyone ever wonder how she can remain so unaffected? A heart of gold they claim, but I say she has no heart at all. Donna the doll, pretty on the outside, hollow on the inside.

To outsiders it appears Donna is oblivious to the adoration and praise bestowed upon her; an angel of mercy, fulfilling destiny's call. Competent and trustworthy in the eyes of administrators and those in higher positions, worshipped and treasured by those who depend on her. But not me, I see through her disguise, I know what she's capable of.

White suits her I must admit, gives her an almost surreal glow, an innocent virginal aura which adds to her masquerade. Even after ten hours on the job she's still as squeaky-clean and neat as when she arrived this morning and she never complains if her workload becomes more than most people could tolerate. Of course she doesn't; this is where Donna most likes to be, this is where she can practice what she does best. She'll often volunteer for extra duty; it keeps her in everyone's good books and gives her more opportunities.

Her name is Donna; it means "A cultured and refined lady." Suits her don't you think? But what no one knows about Donna is that behind that façade she's a manipulative, aggressive and deceptive bitch. She's perfected the art of lying and baffles everyone with the devious ways she covers her tracks. She's an impostor who pretends she needs no reward or praise, when in reality she's screaming for attention. That's why she poisons and paralyses people, it's part of her illness; she may not even be aware of how much suffering she causes.

The majority in here are unaware or so messed up by her lethal injections and concoctions of medication they're unable to understand. I know the truth but you try telling your psychiatrist it's the nurse who's crazy, not you.

Don't

They sit on the bed, huddled together, both close to tears. Their relationship so perfect they can share every problem, fear, and emotion, knowing the other will understand and advise; never judge.

'Mum, I can't go through with it. What shall I do? Should I have an abortion?' The word hits the cool, winter air in the bedroom. A chill lingers.

How can she tell her after all these years? She wants to scream, "Don't do it," but she has kept the secret hidden in her broken heart for too many years now. She shudders. She is back at the clinic, the smell of disinfectant making her want to vomit. Sixteen, pregnant, alone, knowing she cannot share this with anyone close. Once the foetus is removed from her body she believes all will be well. But it isn't. The pain of the abortion is nothing compared to the pain she carries with her every day of her life. The shame, the guilt and the overwhelming sense of loss a daily reminder of her unforgivable crime. How can she tell her distraught daughter that it ruins your life; flushing your unborn child away like a soiled handkerchief. How can she confess that she murdered her daughter's sibling? She cannot.

'Sweetheart, it's your body, your life. It's up to you.' She attempts to smile but her mind still screams, don't do it.

Saved By Music

She arrived on a cattle truck, dishevelled, malnourished, petrified, her trembling hands clutching a small package to her chest.

Interrogation confirmed she carried only a violin. Too young for a lover, music was her passion.

Separated from her travelling companions she was hustled into block number twelve. Others marched away to the sound of a band, though she knew not where. She would not see them again.

In the days that followed she heard the screech of train brakes, the screams of families separated forever, the barking orders of guards, but sometimes music filled the air.

Resentful yet compliant she joined the small orchestra to entertain the villainous guards, the epitome of evil. An orchestra of musical slaves, available at all times, yet granted privileges essential for survival. Flimsy, uncertain protection from the worst of unspeakable evils under the bleakest conditions imaginable.

By day playing music on command to accompany punishments, executions and fool new arrivals marching to an impending fate became her role. Sometimes the smoke from the crematorium was so thick she could barely read the notes. Life disappeared, only music survived.

Yet late at night, by candlelight in tiny rooms, musicians found consolation, support and confidence; reminding them of their earlier lives, helping them articulate feelings and deal with the ever present threats. A way of preserving some dignity where little otherwise existed. A temporary escape.

Musicians and singers among the imprisoned crafted in secret. Symphonies, tangos, operas, folk songs, waltzes, gypsy tunes, love songs scribbled in charcoal given as dysentery medicine. Arrangements penned on food wrappings, telegrams, potato sacks or toilet paper. An explosion of creativity; composing and performing assisted in alleviating the terror.

Years later she was transported from the camp, leaving behind mountains of shoes, suitcases, glasses, shaving brushes, corpses. She would never lose the scars, the harrowing memories or the numbers tattooed on her left arm, but still clutched the violin wrapped inside hidden masterpieces. Music saved her.

Decades later the world hears the music composed in captivity then smuggled out into the world. Music that could have been destroyed or lost but has now been freed. Carefully revived, catalogued, liberated documents infested with paper worms, rescued from anonymity and decay. Dedicated, skilful researchers breathed life back into lost masterpieces that may have changed the world. Now no one can take it away. No one can imprison it. Their music has been saved.

Tying The Knot

I help fasten your black tie. You force the zip of my too tight dress.

We tie the knot at four in the afternoon. Exchange rings and vows. Promise to love and honour. As long as we both shall live. Two become one, bound together.

We share everything. Love notes, showers, long walks, bedtimes, lingering kisses, prayers, bucket lists, compliments, household chores, chocolates, inside jokes, struggles, credit cards, laughter and tears. We cherish our equality, value our mutual respect, treasure our precious time.

The knot loosens. Tensions build. You book the tables. I pay the bills. You go out alone. I stay home. You gain new friends. I'm not allowed any. You expose my weaknesses. I hide my hurt. You win every argument. I lose my self esteem.

The rope begins to fray. I slave in the kitchen. You slob out watching sport. I ask questions. You don't answer. I buy wine. You drink it. I remember our anniversary. You forget to buy roses. I accept your excuses. You reject my advances.

The rope strains. You eat out. I order takeaways. You don't come home. I sleep alone. You raise your voice. I lower my gaze. You laugh in public. I cry in private. You yell. I whimper. You lash out. I bruise. You deny it's intentional. I claim it's an accident.

Our life on a tightrope. We're a tangled mess. You are a parasite. I will not be your host. At four in the afternoon I tie the knot. Place the chair beneath the tightened noose. I am taking back control. I will have the last word. Fasten your own black tie.

ANOTHER SMALL PRESS

A selection of titles available from www.anothersmallpress.net

Laura Lee Dove

NAILING JELLY TO THE CEILING

Life is full of possibilities, we're told. We are encouraged to reach out and grasp them. But what happens when life seems to present us with an overload of impossibilities? For some of us, all we can do is try to cling on as we slowly and painfully lose our grasp on life itself. There are some things we just cannot control. Nailing Jelly To The Ceiling searingly illustrates this truth, whether you believe it or not. It is a deeply personal, brutally honest account of painful events that impacted the author's life over a long period of time.

Mental health is a complex, diverse subject and despite positive anti-stigma campaigning and acceptance discourse prevalent in modern culture, often remains an unwelcome topic for discussion. The reality of living with mental illness is not easily put into words, but Laura Lee Dove has achieved precisely that, nurturing understanding and support for both those who suffer as well as those who don't.

£9.99

Adrian Bean

WHAT HAPPENED

'RAF Syerston - that's where your uncle George's brother died
during the war.'
'What happened?'
'I don't know...'

A short but intriguing conversation about a relative who died
in a wartime plane crash started Adrian Bean on a journey that
would obsess him for nearly two years. Curiosity, as well as a
fascination with aeroplanes and the Second World War drove
him to ask who was this relative and why had he never known
of his existence? How did he die, and why? And what was the
link with a wartime RAF bomber station and the Polish
bomber crews who flew from there?

   He would also come to ask deeper questions, not just about
what happened in June 1941 but more recently, about the
break-up of his own family, and just what it was that was
driving him to find answers.

   Sometimes funny, often disturbing, always honest, What
Happened is a book about loss, and acceptance, not only in
wartime; it is about discovery and memory and how we create
and tell stories about the past to make sense of our own
present.

£9.99

Martin Costello

ALL THE THINGS I WROTE BEFORE I WROTE THE THING I ALWAYS WANTED TO WRITE

Eight picaresque ballads of life in the East Midlands - and sometimes on the seashore - by mild mannered anarchist & writer Martin Costello.

The elder boys carried the old sofa to the end of the pier, and the family set it up looking outward across the water so that they might catch an early sight of the ferry. They took turns on the watch through the long late afternoon, the children happily amusing themselves on the pier, under the pier, behind the sofa, in the mud, in the shallows, in the empty car park, on the roof of the ticket hut, up and down the ferry lane, along the grassy dunes of the strand, on the smooth round rocks of the tide wall and around the skirts of the mother Bidna to her passing amusement and then impatience and then amusement again. As evening threatened, a dog-walker from the lane helpfully called out that there would be no ferries that day, on account of the coming storm.

The story the author had always been trying to write is not included in this collection but happily is now complete after 22 years of editing.

£7.99

Lynn Roulstone

NOTTINGHAM SWING

In Victorian London a housekeeper recounts the story of a puzzling encounter with a young man, while in Victorian Newark a local businessman thinks he's got away with murder.

Meanwhile in modern day London a troll (the fairy book kind) mourns the passing of his traditional lifestyle as he searches for his lost love, while one teacher has a bad start to his day, and another mourns the loss of his career.

Would Dorothy's life have been different if she'd cut her hair earlier, would Carrie have been happier if she hadn't deliberately tripped up her dance partner at a ceilidh. Should Lilian open the kitbag she finds in her understairs cupboard, and is Laura pinning too much on her relationship with her new neighbour?

This selection of stories by Newark author Lynn Roulstone travels in time from medieval Newark to present day Italy, but they all have a common theme of choices not made, paths not taken.

£7.99

Kathryn Fox

THREE FIELDS AND A RIVER

An autobiographical collection arranged in sections relating to the stages of life - early childhood, young adulthood and into the present day. Poems spring from events, memories, and people. Themes of time, loss, responsibility, freedom, the relationship between parents and children, mothers and daughters and the enduring love within a long marriage occur and reoccur.

Kath Fox writes her poetry at the dining room table as family life ebbs and flows around her and inevitably influences the themes of her poems, often exploring domestic and family life. Her poems are humane and generous, laced with a lilting longing for the past. She revisits people and places with tranquillity and gentleness but does not flinch from exposing the emotional truths she uncovers in her reflections.

The river weaves its way through all the sections, representing creativity; the silver thread connecting the past, the present and the future.

£7.99

Printed and bound by CPI Group (UK) Ltd, Croydon, CR0 4YY

04/07/2025

01910812-0001